ROSIE
IN LOS ANGELES
Action!

BY CAROL MATAS

ALADDIN PAPERBACKS

NEW YORK LONDON TORONTO SYDNEY

For Brenda Barrie,
who also loves California

First Aladdin Paperbacks edition February 2004

Copyright © 2004 by Carol Matas

ALADDIN PAPERBACKS
An imprint of Simon & Schuster
Children's Publishing Division
1230 Avenue of the Americas
New York, NY 10020

Designed by Sammy Yuen Jr.
The text of this book was set in Utopia.

Printed in the United States of America
2 4 6 8 10 9 7 5 3 1

Library of Congress Control Number 2003105622

ISBN 0-689-85716-0

Chapter 1

"Rosie!"

"What?"

Abe was motioning me to hurry over. I was floating in the sky, though, so that wasn't easy.

"Look!" Abe exclaimed. "A cowboy!"

"*Shalom*, y'all," a tall man in a Stetson said to me. He was floating too.

Suddenly I jerked awake. I must have dozed off. I was on the back porch, curled up in a long, over-stuffed settee that had been rigged so it could swing back and forth. What a very odd dream. And what did that word *shalom* mean? It sounded familiar, but I couldn't place it.

I stared out at the breathtakingly beautiful view. An expanse of flat ground covered in chaparral gave way to the foothills of the Santa Monica Mountains, which were directly behind our little ranch. A black phoebe fought with a wren for the same branch. Or perhaps they were playing? The wren flew to a higher branch and began to sing. I was thrilled, as if I were the only patron at a very special concert.

"Rosie!" Abe ran over to me, scaring both birds away.

"Now look what you've done," I scolded Abe.

"I've been calling and calling! Didn't you hear me?" He grabbed my arm and began to pull me.

"What?" I protested.

He dragged me around the side of the house so I was able to see the road that led to our ranch.

"You're not going to believe your eyes," Abe declared.

I hadn't been able to believe my eyes since we'd arrived in California. I remember when the train drew near Los Angeles, I saw the orange trees. Trees with fruit growing on them! Honestly, I had believed that fruit grew in boxes in the peddlers' pushcarts on Maxwell Street in Chicago or Orchard Street in New York. And the flowers! Everywhere there was a riot of color. Then when we disembarked, I marveled at the heat of the sun and the blue skies in January! I felt like I was dreaming.

Once again, I had that strange sensation. Was this another dream? Because on the road in front of our home I saw a long line of people riding in trucks and on horseback, but they weren't just any kind of people. They were cowboys and cowgirls! They wore Stetsons on their heads, chaps on their legs, and spurs on their cowboy boots. They rode magnificent horses that kicked up the dust on the road, making the entire party look like it was veiled in a fog of fairy dust.

I clapped my hands together. *"Oy veysmere!"* I exclaimed.

"Papa's only gone and hired an entire Wild West show for the movies," Abe announced.

I stared at my younger brother. "He hasn't!"

Mama and Joe walked up from behind us.

"Oh yes, he has," Mama said. "Now Joe," she warned, "you stay well away from those horses."

"Mama, eight years old is old enough to ride a horse," Joe objected. "Not that I'd *want* to."

I grinned. I couldn't imagine Joe on a horse—reading about them was much more like him.

Joe looked up at me. "I'm not sure *you'll* be smiling like that the first time you have to get on one, Rosie," he commented.

A rush of fear zigzagged down my back. But fear and I were not partners. I quickly shook it off and kept smiling. "It'll be exciting, that's all," I retorted.

"And don't forget me," Abe said. "Papa promised

I could be in the film too, and I'll get to ride a horse! I can't wait. Although," he added, "they *are* awfully big and tall, aren't they? I mean when you're so close."

"Nonsense," I scoffed. "You've seen plenty of horses on Orchard Street."

"True," Abe said, "but I never thought about riding on one."

"I did," I declared. "I imagined being a cowgirl and a sharpshooter like Annie Oakley. Now *that's* adventure!"

"They're going to set up camp over there," Mama said, pointing to the large field right near our house. It was covered only in wild grasses and some small bushes.

"For how long?" I asked.

"A few months at least," Mama answered. "Papa wants to do a new movie every week. He met the troupe when they were doing a show in Chicago."

I remembered Papa coming back from seeing their show last year. The rest of us hadn't been able to go because it was too expensive.

Mama continued, "Papa has been corresponding with them ever since. They came to California around the same time we did to rest for the winter, and were about to leave to go on tour when Papa offered them this job. They didn't have very many bookings for their tour, so this seemed like a good financial choice for them."

Suddenly I saw Papa waving to us from the front seat of his new truck. He tooted the horn, sending the horses into neighs and prances. When he'd first come home with the truck, so slick and shiny, in a bright and cheery yellow with red wheels, I couldn't imagine a bigger surprise. But this was certainly bigger.

California was just full of surprises, really. When we first arrived, Papa had wanted to buy a perfect little house in a part of Los Angeles called Hollywood. But there were signs everywhere that read JEWS AND ACTORS NOT ALLOWED. Since we were Jews *and* in the movie business, that ruled us out! We stayed in a boarding house in downtown Los Angeles for a week until Papa came home one night and said, "We're changing our name. If we don't have a Jewish-sounding name we'll be able to buy land with no one asking any funny questions."

We had a family conference and everyone suggested a variation on Lepidus. Mama suggested Lep, Abe suggested Pie, Papa thought maybe Lorris, I came up with Idus, and then Joe piped up with Lake. We all laughed until it occurred to us that Lake was a pretty good name. And so I became Rosie

Lake. I felt sad to have to say good-bye to our name, but Papa said we could start using it again as soon as Jews became more accepted in Hollywood.

It was such a perfect place to film, he said; with the Santa Monica Mountains right there, the setting was perfect for Westerns. And so within two weeks of our arrival we were living on a small ranch in Los Angeles, in the district called Hollywood.

The house had four bedrooms. Four! I had my own room for the first time in my life. There was a sitting room in the back of the house, a large kitchen, a front parlor, a back porch, *and* a front porch. Imagine! Our entire apartment on Orchard Street in New York could probably fit in the kitchen and sitting room in our new home!

At first all I wanted to do was sit and stare at the lemon tree in our front yard and smell the flowers. My freckled face soon showed that I was getting far too much sun.

Mama had to teach us at home every day, as Papa had us acting in the movies he made all winter. Often Mama left me in charge while she went to suffragette meetings. An important vote was coming up in California, and Mama, just as she had in New York and Chicago, was working hard for women to gain the right to vote.

When Papa filmed his first movie in Chicago we all thought it was just a practice film, but it was shipped to New York by mistake where his partner distributed it. It told the story of a baseball game. I played in the outfield dressed as a boy—until the end of the movie when my hat fell off to reveal that I was really a girl. The public loved it and it became a surprise hit. Papa made more films like it with me playing different sports, always pretending to be a boy. But then Papa decided we needed a new twist on the stories.

"Westerns!" he'd declared one night. "Westerns. You'll pretend to be a boy, Rosie—riding and all— and then off will come your cowboy hat and you'll be you. People can't get enough of that story."

"You'd think they'd be bored by now," Joe said, "since they know the ending."

"Not at all," Papa grinned. "They look forward to the ending. But they *are* getting bored with the sports. None of us, and none of the actors I've been using, can ride horses, though," he mused. "Never mind. I'll think of something!"

And he certainly had! It was a small Wild West show compared to the huge Miller's 101 Ranch show—that one must have had hundreds of performers, as well as wild animals, horses, bulls, and cattle. This one had perhaps thirty people that I could see heading our way, and maybe ten horses. I watched in amazement as they stopped in the nearby field and began putting up their tents.

"I wonder what your Papa agreed to pay them," Mama muttered as she hurried off to meet and welcome the troupe. Mama had become the manager of the film company, and she took care of all the business. Abe and Joe followed me as I hurried right after Mama.

"Out of the way, youngins," was the first thing the three of us heard from one of the members of the troupe. The horses were stomping impatiently, and as I tried to find Papa I had to be careful that they didn't stomp on me.

Suddenly someone pushed me roughly to one side. "Hey!" I protested.

"Hey, yourself." I turned to see a boy scowling at me. "You three trying to get yourselves killed?" he asked.

"No," I said, scowling back.

"Well, you will without trying," he said. "Or you'll spook one of the horses. Now get out of our way."

"We don't have to listen to you," I protested.

"You'd best," he retorted.

He was a tall, lanky boy. And he had the most unusual mark on his forehead. It began just above one eyebrow, curved up on his forehead, and dropped down to his other eyebrow, like a large upside-down U. His face was tanned a deep brown, but the mark on his forehead stood out in pale white.

Joe tugged at my blouse. "We'd better listen to him, Rosie," he said. "Come on."

Reluctantly I allowed Joe and Abe to lead me back to the porch, out of the way of the chaos of the troupe.

"We can visit once they're set up," Abe assured me.

In no time I'd forgotten about the boy with the strange mark and all I could think about was how exciting it was going to be to make a Western. *Rosie Lake, Western star!*

We sat on the front porch and watched the tents go up, the horses get unsaddled, the boys run back and forth to our well for water, and the general hubbub caused by such a large group settling in. Joe said, "I'm not sure this will be any safer than the last movies we made."

I gave him a gentle push.

"You shouldn't worry so much about safety," I chided him.

"Well, *someone* in this family has to," he said, defending himself.

I knew what he was referring to, of course. Papa had simply used whatever was happening in the city as part of the picture for many of the films he had made. For instance, Papa filmed a story about me being a champion runner. In the movie I secretly believed I could beat any boy, except none would race a girl. So I dressed up like a boy and then raced the boys—and won! When they discovered I was a girl they were so mad they chased me.

Papa arranged to film that scene when there was a parade marching downtown. He trained the camera on the parade, and then I ran into the marchers, followed by Abe, who played one of the boys chasing me. The young men in the marching band glanced at us askance but couldn't break step to do anything about us. We marched along for a couple of minutes, trying to look as silly as possible. Finally we ran off and mingled with the crowd. Papa turned the camera and started filming us in the crowd until a policeman yelled, "Hey you! What are you doing?"

In no time Papa had unhooked the camera from the tripod, Mama had grabbed one part, Papa had grabbed the other, and they were dodging in and out of the crowd, trying to get lost in it. And so were we!

That wasn't the only time the police had chased us. Perhaps horses would be safer by comparison.

As the day drew to a close we saw campfires flickering and smelled meat roasting. I was tired from staring for so long from so far away. Just when I thought it finally might be safe to go over, Mama called me to help her prepare our dinner.

I was so anxious to question Papa about everything, I could barely contain myself as I worked in the kitchen. I peeled the potatoes and put them on to boil, put a carrot and date compote on the stove to simmer, and peeled fresh avocados. Food seemed to taste better here, probably because it was so fresh—it was often just off the trees or out of the ground. I could smell the chicken roasting, and I was starting to get hungry.

Finally Papa arrived for dinner. As we sat around the table I asked him, "Do you have a story written for the film already, Papa?"

"Not yet, Rosie," he answered. "I need to talk to each of the members of the troupe, and to find out what their areas of expertise are. I'm sure, though, that they all ride, so I suspect this story will be centered around that. Maybe it will involve a group of cattle rustlers." He thought for a moment. "But I don't have cattle."

"What about bank robbers?" I suggested.

His eyes lit up.

"That's a good idea, Rosie. We could build a set of a Western town and then have the robbers ride off into the hills. We could use the set for all the pictures."

"What would my role be, Papa?" I asked.

He thought for a moment. "Maybe you could be the daughter of the bank robber. He forces you to be bad. But one day you reveal yourself to the son of the sheriff, and he helps you escape."

"Can I be the sheriff's son?" Abe asked.

"Abe, I'll find a part for you, but I think we'll need a youngster who can really ride for that part," Papa said.

Abe looked disappointed. "You could be the younger brother of the lead character," Papa offered. "Don't worry, there will be other stories for you, Abe."

"What are they like?" I asked him.

"They?"

"The cowboys," I answered.

"They seem like fine people," Papa replied. "Very hardworking. They've fallen on hard times. Most are real cowboys who can't get work on the ranches or cattle drives anymore. That's almost a way of life that's gone forever, so they join together and do these Wild West shows. But it's a hard living if you aren't in one of the big shows. They perform at small county fairs, and travel all the time."

Just then there was a knock at the kitchen door.

Mama hurried to answer it. I heard her talking. She came back smiling.

"That was Mrs. Brady. She wanted to thank me for the greens. Said they hadn't eaten anything that had color for weeks. I'll make sure they're all healthy before they leave here," Mama said, determined. And I knew she would.

"When can I try riding a horse, Papa?" I asked.

"Tomorrow, Rosie," Papa answered.

"I won't sleep a wink tonight," I pronounced.

"Lucky for you then," Abe said, "that you napped all the morning away!"

Let him tease, I thought. *Tomorrow I'll learn to ride a horse!* I couldn't wait.

Chapter 2

I DID SLEEP, THOUGH. I SLEPT SO SOUNDLY THAT WHEN I WOKE up and hurried out of the kitchen, Papa was already gone. Abe and Joe were nowhere to be seen. Before I could speak, Mama did.

"Good morning, sleepyhead."

"Where is everyone?"

"Papa has gone to visit the troupe. He wants to see what each person can do. Joe and Abe are on the back porch doing their reading. Which is where you are going as soon as you've eaten."

"But Mama—"

"Don't 'but Mama' me. There are always good reasons not to study. Your Papa has agreed with me that until he begins filming, you three will do your studies every morning."

"But I'm supposed to learn to ride today!"

"And you will. But first things first. 'If a man has

knowledge, he has all things; if he has no knowledge, he has nothing.'"

I sighed. When Mama started quoting there was no point in arguing with her. Her mind was made up. I made a point of not asking her where the quote was from, because that would only result in a much longer lecture.

Mama made sure I was settled on the back porch at the small table before she hurried off to help Papa. To learn the art of letter writing, I was to produce a sample letter for her. Abe and Joe were doing mathematics. I decided that if I had to write a letter I would write a formal one to two of my friends—first to Maria in New York, and then to Carl in Chicago. As I followed the instructions in the book, however, my mind wandered. When would I start my training for the movie?

I stared up at the black phoebe in the oak tree, then looked down at the table. The sun made dappled spots on my paper, and instead of writing, I began tracing them with my pen. The black phoebe sang. I pictured myself galloping along the wide streets of Hollywood, the prim and proper inhabitants, parasols clutched in their hands, fleeing in fear as I rode past. Our ranch was only a block from streets lined neatly with brilliant red bougainvilleas, orange California poppies, yellow snapdragons, purple pansies, and countless other varieties of flowers. Hollywood was mad for flowers. Unfortunately, my magnificent steed would trample the flowers underfoot as he rose up and then crashed to the ground. The women and girls would scream in dismay as I shot my gun in the air. . . .

"Rosie. Rosie!"

I looked over to see Abe grinning at me. "You aren't working. Mama won't be too pleased with you."

I looked at my paper and noticed the mess I'd made. "She won't be too pleased with this, either," I said. I crumpled the paper and took a fresh piece from the package Mama had left.

"You are setting a dreadful example, Rosie," Joe commented.

"You don't need an example, fortunately," I assured him. "You'd study even if I were setting a much worse example—if I were a criminal, for instance."

"You will be," Abe reminded me. "In the movie."

"Yes, and I need to practice criminal behavior." I grinned.

"I hardly think wasting paper would be considered criminal," Joe said. "Now quiet. This is a difficult problem I'm working on."

Properly scolded by my younger brother, I settled down and wrote two letters to my friends filled with all my exciting news. I'd been so busy with filming I'd been very bad about my letter writing over the last month or so.

When the letters were finished, Mama had not returned, and I could stand it no longer—I *had* to go see what was happening in the cowboy camp. Just as I was folding up my letters Papa burst onto the porch. Papa, who is very tall, with red hair like mine and a deep booming voice, never creeps up on a person.

"Wonderful news!" he exclaimed.

"What, Papa?"

"There's a man in the troupe who bills himself as 'the Cowboy King.' His name is actually Billy King. He does all the trick riding we'll need for the story. After lunch, the whole troupe will put on a small show for us so we can see how we can write them into the story. Now, you three stay out of trouble. Mama and I have to go to the bank. I'm going to need a loan in order to build the set. And somehow I have to figure out how to get wood for it." He waved at the hills. "No trees for us to cut down there." Without waiting for a word from us he turned and left.

Papa was right about the trees. The hills were

covered in bushes. Mama had explained that was because there wasn't enough rain to support most trees in this climate. Those that were here, such as the oak or pines, would be too difficult to get to, as they were far up in the hills.

"He doesn't think we're really going to stay here, does he?" I said to my brothers.

"*I* am," Joe replied. "All those horses and such! No, I'll just stay right here." He put away his mathematics and brought out a new book. I could see it was the latest novel by L. Frank Baum.

I looked at Abe.

"Wait five minutes until Papa and Mama are gone," Abe said.

I nodded. For the next five minutes I paced. Finally I heard the truck chugging away from the house.

"Come on!" I said to Abe.

We raced around the house and in no time were at the camp. But before we could explore and try to meet people the boy with the scar was there blocking our way. He stood, arms folded, a slight frown on his face.

"We're getting ready for our show," he said. "You can't come in now. You can see it all this afternoon."

"We won't get in the way," I spluttered, indignant.

"No, you won't," he agreed. "Now scat!"

Scat? I wasn't a cat, was I? "Hmmph," I grunted. What was I going to answer? *You* scat? That would be too childish. So I simply stuck my nose in the air, turned my back on the boy, and began to saunter off as if I didn't care. I heard Abe behind me.

"Come on. Please. We just want to look at the horses."

"You'll see them soon enough," I heard the boy answer.

"I'll let you try my baseball glove," Abe said.

I turned around to see how the boy would react. He paused a minute. He looked tempted.

"Naw," he said finally. "I'd get in trouble up to my neck. But thanks. I gotta go help." At that he turned and started back into the camp. They had set up the camp so that the tents were close to our house. Behind them, toward the hills and the pastures, the horses were in a large pen. There was a barn beside the house, but they didn't seem to be using it.

Abe and I headed back to the house. "I know what you're thinking, Rosie," Abe said.

"You do not," I said.

"I do. You're thinking that you'll wait until that boy is gone and then sneak back. I don't think you should, Rosie."

"Why?" I asked defiantly.

"They obviously don't want us underfoot. After lunch we'll see the show. We should wait."

I kicked the dirt on the path back to the house. "All right," I agreed reluctantly.

The time dragged on until Papa and Mama finally returned from the bank. By then I had fed the boys their lunch and set out food for Mama and Papa.

"This looks lovely, Rosie," Mama said with a smile as she and Papa washed at the sink. "Have you eaten?"

"Who can eat?" I asked. "I can't wait until the show."

"Eat!" Mama insisted.

I managed to swallow a cut-up hard boiled egg on a piece of rye bread spread thick with butter. I washed it down with fresh lemonade that I kept in a pitcher for myself. It had no sugar added, and no one else could drink it. It was funny to see their mouths pucker up when they tried. But I loved it.

Finally it was time to go see the show. Papa carried two folding chairs for himself and Mama. We followed him along the path from our house to the pasture. At the entrance to the little city of tents, that boy strode up to us. This time he greeted us politely and said, "This way, please."

We walked along the path, between tents on either side. Among the tents were cooking fires and signs of a camp settling in: laundry hung to dry, food stuffs set up, a few young children playing marbles. I supposed they washed their clothes in the tubs I saw here or there, filled with water Mama had told them to take from the pump at the back of the house. Behind the small camp was the pen in which the horses were kept, but now the pen was empty. I could see the troupe in the open ground behind the pen. It was a long stretch of land—perhaps an acre—that reached all the way to the foothills, but the troupe had cordoned off part of it with festive poles and ribbons. The horses neighed and stomped as their riders awaited our arrival.

Papa put down the chairs and he and Mama sat down. We sat near them on the ground.

There were two lines of riders, all dressed in their finest cowboy gear. They had rifles under their arms or six-shooters in their holsters. The two lines faced each other. One man raised his hand, then let it fall. The riders spurred their horses and the horses charged. The horses pounded the ground, and for a moment I was sure they were going to crash right into each other, but at the last second one of the lines swerved and charged past the other.

As they pulled their horses up we all clapped enthu-siastically.

Then the riders formed a large circle and each one took a turn doing something quite spectacular. The first fellow rode his horse at a gallop around and around. As he did so another rider, still mounted, stood on his saddle, balanced, and threw a ball into the air. The first rider pulled out his six-gun and shot. The ball splintered into little pieces. This time we cheered!

A cowgirl riding in pants on a man's saddle—not a sidesaddle—took her turn next. She rode her horse at full speed while she dropped first onto one side of the saddle, next onto the other side, then backward. After that she stood straight up, balanc-ing on the saddle. With one hand, she drew a small ball from her pocket. With the other, she drew her gun. She threw the ball into the air, the horse turned at a full gallop, and she shot the ball into little pieces. I couldn't believe my eyes!

A cowboy followed her. He had a rifle under his arm. Another fellow took a pile of clay pigeons from a sack on his saddle and began to throw them, one after another, as fast as he could, into the sky. And one after another the rider shot them from the sky.

My heart was pounding so fast with each new

amazing feat I thought it would jump out of my chest. I glanced at Abe and Joe. Their jaws had dropped open and they stared with wide eyes. Mama had her hand over her mouth, and Papa was beaming from ear to ear, smiling as though he were in the middle of a candy shop. He noticed me looking at him.

"What do you think, Rosie?" he asked. "Will they be good in our movie?"

"Good, Papa? They'll make every Western filmed up until now look foolish. This will be so real, so true. Papa, people will love it!"

"You'll have a lot of work to do to keep up," Papa noted.

"You don't need me to ride like *that*, do you?" I asked.

Papa laughed. "No, Rosie. If you can just stay on a horse we can make you look good by having all the fancy riding done around you."

Our attention was quickly drawn back to the riders as the boy we'd met earlier ran into the circle. He held up a red handkerchief, then dropped it on the ground. A cowboy rode his horse slowly around the other horses, then picked up speed. Once he was moving very quickly, he headed straight for the handkerchief, dropped to the side of the horse, and scooped it up, the horse never breaking its stride. Letting go of the reins altogether, he tied the handkerchief around his neck while the horse continued its gallop.

Again we cheered.

After that the riders took their horses into trots and an intricate dance followed, the horses moving in and out in a wonderful pattern, never out of step. When this was finished they lined up facing us and each horse took an individual bow, bending one leg while the riders took off their hats.

Mama and Papa stood up, as did we children, and we all clapped. "Wonderful!" Papa called. "Wonderful!"

The rider who had done the handkerchief trick jumped off his horse and came over to us.

"Children," Papa said, "this is Mr. Billy King, otherwise known as 'the Cowboy King.'"

Mr. King bowed again and looked at us all. "Is this the young star?" he asked, looking at me.

"It is," Papa said.

I think my cheeks were probably as red as my hair. Star? Me?

"You ready to learn to ride, Miss Rosie?"

"You bet I am!" I declared.

He smiled. "Good for you. No time like the

present. But perhaps you'd like to put on a pair of pants?"

All I had were the breeches that Papa had let me wear when I was an usher. I looked at Mama.

"Don't worry, Rosie, I thought about this already. I stopped at the store this morning and bought you a pair of overalls."

"Really, Mama?" Now I'd be like a true ranch hand.

"Go on. I left them on your bed."

I turned and raced as fast I could back to the house. In no time I was dressed in my new overalls. I took a moment to look at myself in the mirror in my room. I *did* look like a ranch hand. I couldn't wait to get onto a horse.

Chapter 3

By the time I returned to the camp, most of the riders were off their horses, removing the saddles and brushing the horses down. I hoped that soon I'd be taught how to help care for the horses—they were such graceful, striking animals.

Soon I'd be playing an outlaw. As I ran to join Mama and Papa, I began to practice my role, pretending to duck and shoot. I darted into the circle where they were waiting, the Cowboy King back on his horse. I spun around and shouted, "Bang! Bang!"

The Cowboy King's horse reared back at my sudden entrance, and the Cowboy King, who'd been deep in conversation with Papa and wasn't even holding the horse's reins, fell off his horse!

No one paid much attention at first. I think everyone assumed he'd just get up, because the riders had accidents all the time. But he didn't move.

When the horse put its nose down and nudged the Cowboy King, he shrieked in pain. This caused everyone to suddenly stop what they were doing and stare in horror.

"Don't move," Mama ordered. "Roy, you must go fetch the doctor."

Papa nodded, then turned and ran for the truck. Mama bent over Mr. King as others from his troupe began gathering around.

"Never heard Billy cry out loud like that," said a female sharpshooter to Mama.

Mama looked up. "I'm afraid he's broken his leg."

I crept over to look. Sure enough, a piece of his bone was sticking out through his pants. It was dreadful. I felt a little woozy, so I sat down right where I was.

"Billy?" Bella, the sharpshooter, said. "You okay?"

Billy managed a grunt in reply. And then, "I'll be fine."

I couldn't believe he wasn't crying like a baby. I would have been doing that *and* shrieking in agony. He certainly was brave!

"Is there a Mrs. King?" Mama asked.

"Nope. She died some years ago," Bella answered. "Just him and Zach."

"Zach?"

"The boy. Here he is."

The boy with the scar pushed everyone aside and knelt by the Cowboy King—his father.

"Pa?" he said, looking at his father's leg. "That doesn't look good."

"Then don't look at it," Billy said, trying to joke.

"We shouldn't move him until the doctor arrives," Mama decided. "Rosie, run to the house and get a blanket and a glass of water."

"I'll help her," Abe offered.

He and I rushed back to the house, Abe chastising me as we went. "That was a whopper of a thing to do," he said.

"I just got carried away, imagining the film! I thought those horses were so well trained I didn't have to worry."

Abe snorted. "They're horses, not people. Even if they're well trained, they'll startle if you scare them."

By now we were at the house. "You get the water," I told him, "and I'll get the blanket."

We hurried back with both. Mama tried to make Mr. King as comfortable as she could. Finally Papa returned with the doctor. He was a young man with a small black mustache, a neat black suit, and a brisk manner.

"I'm going to have to set this leg, but I don't want to do it here in the open in the middle of all this dirt and dust," he stated. "Can we use a room in the house?"

Mama said, "Of course. Perhaps the table in the kitchen?"

"Can you boil water and get me some clean linen?"

"I can," Mama answered.

"We'll need to make a stretcher to move him."

"We have one," Bella answered. "This ain't the first time we've needed one, and I know it won't be the last."

Moving him onto the stretcher was tricky. He passed out just before we reached the house, from the pain, I guess, although he never so much as let out a moan. Mama sent me away, so I didn't see the doctor at work.

Zach stood at the bottom of the front steps that led up to the porch, looking uncertain about what he should be doing.

"You'd better come up here and wait with us," Abe said.

Zach nodded. Joe was already sitting on a chair in the corner.

"Just a minute," Abe said. He ran into the

house, then came out with his catcher's mitt and a ball.

"Want to try it?"

Zach nodded. "Sure."

Abe took the ball and he and Zach went down to the front lawn. They played catch. It seemed to help take Zach's mind off his father. Sometimes Abe is pretty clever.

I sat down in the chair beside Joe.

"Don't be too hard on yourself, Rosie," Joe said. "You didn't mean to hurt him."

"I was stupid," I said, dropping my head into my hands.

"You were excited," Joe said. "Those horses are used to loud shouts, gunshots, and all sorts of sudden noises. And so are the riders. That's why you'd call this an accident."

I leaned over and kissed Joe on the cheek.

"That wasn't necessary," Joe complained, wiping his cheek.

"Yes, it was," I answered.

The members of the troupe stayed in their camp, busying themselves with their chores.

Finally Mama came outside. She called Zach over.

"Zach," she said, "the doctor has finished with

your father. He seems to be a very good doctor. But your dad won't be riding horses for at least two months."

"Thanks, ma'am," Zach said.

"Rosie, fix some lemonade for the doctor and Zach, please," Mama said.

Soon a few of the cowboys came over. They brought crutches for Mr. King so that he could return with them to camp, but Mama would have none of it. "He's sleeping right here in the house for the next few days," she said. "He can't be in a tent. Zach, you can stay in the same room and help take care of him."

Zach nodded his head.

In no time Mama had the house organized for our new guest, turning the sitting room into a bedroom and putting me to work cooking a soup for Mr. King's supper.

When we finally sat down for our own supper, Mr. King was asleep. Zach joined us.

"Guess you'll have to take over his tricks in the movie," Papa said to Zach. "Your father wasn't too sick to tell me that you can do them as well as he can."

Zach nodded.

"Can you ride like that?" Abe asked.

"I can," Zach said. But he didn't say any more.

We tried to make conversation but it was hard with Zach sitting there looking so glum. And I felt pretty glum myself. And guilty.

After dinner we children were sent to bed early. Papa wanted to get started at dawn the next day finding the wood for the set. And Zach would give me my first riding lesson.

That night I had a terrible time falling asleep. When I finally did I had a very strange dream. The same cowboy I'd dreamed about before appeared on a horse riding out of a beautiful sunset.

"Shalom!" he called to me. "Thy own deeds make thy friends or thy enemies."

"Why are you telling me that?" I asked.

"Isn't it obvious?"

I suddenly woke up to a dark room. How could I be dreaming things I didn't even understand? It took me a long time to get back to sleep.

"Papa?" I asked at the breakfast table the next morning, still feeling a little groggy.

"Yes, Rosie."

"What does *shalom* mean?"

Zach walked into the room then.

"Ah, Zach. How is your pa?" Mama asked.

"He's restin' comfortable enough," Zach answered.

"Well, you sit down now and eat with us. I'm making your pa tea and hot bread," she said. "I'm putting plenty of preserves on it. He'll need his strength."

"Mama, you'll make him so fat he'll never ride a horse again," I teased her.

She gave me a look, then made sure Zach sat down.

"In answer to your question, Rosie," Papa answered, "*Shalom* is Hebrew and it means 'hello,' 'good-bye,' and 'peace.'"

"How can it mean all three?" Joe asked, intrigued.

"It just does," Papa answered. "Why do you ask, Rosie?"

"I dreamed it," I replied.

"Dreamed it?" Papa asked. He looked like he was about to ask me something else, but a knock at the door interrupted us. It was Tom, the carpenter who was in charge of building the set.

Papa bustled off to join Tom. "Have fun with your riding lesson, Rosie," he called to me.

"I will, Papa," I called back. I grinned at Zach. "I can't wait."

Zach continued to eat his porridge. He obviously *could* wait. It seemed to me, in fact, that he took forever to get ready. He fed his father, took him to the bathroom, and continued to hang around until finally I cornered the two of them in the sitting room. I needed to speak to Zach's father—I had to apologize to him.

"Hello, Mr. King," I said. "How are you today?"

"Better, Rosie."

"I'm terribly sorry, sir."

"These things happen," he said. "Now you two best go to work."

"I agree," I said. "Are you ready, Zach?"

"I guess."

"Zach," his pa said, giving him a stern look. "You *got* to be ready."

"Yes, Pa, I know."

"So git."

With that, Zach led me through the camp to the corral. He seemed miserable. Maybe he was such a great rider he didn't want to bother teaching me. I couldn't blame him, really. Especially after what I'd done to his father.

As we walked through the camp to the pen we found the campsite deserted. "Where is everyone?" I asked.

"They've all gone into town for supplies and costume fittings," Zach said.

At least I won't have to make a fool of myself in front of too many people, I thought. That was a relief.

When we reached the pen he pointed out a chestnut horse to me.

"That's Star Fire," he said. "See that mark on her forehead?"

I did. It looked like a white star. "She's beautiful, isn't she?" I asked.

"She's also real sweet tempered," Zach said. "Mostly."

"Mostly?"

"Any horse can lash out if it's taken by surprise."

I glanced at his forehead.

"Is that what happened to you?"

He glared at me. "That's none of your business, is it?"

He wasn't easy to make friends with, that was for sure.

"No, I suppose it isn't."

"Well, first you'd best watch me while I saddle her. Then you can walk her around the pen."

He fetched her saddle, the bit for her mouth, and the reins from a tent that had been put up near the corral. Watching him saddle the horse was fascinating. He expertly cinched and tightened everything, talking so fast as he worked that I could barely follow. Star Fire stood quietly the entire time.

"There," he said. "Done."

"I know you've probably never taught anyone before," I said. "But the thing is, you have to go more slowly. I hardly followed any of that. I could never do it by myself."

He turned to me and sighed.

"All right. After lunch I'll take you through it step by step. In the meantime, you get on." He walked the horse away from the others in the pen and waited.

"How?" I asked him.

He pointed to the stirrup. "Put your foot in there, grab the horn on the saddle, and pull yourself up. You need to swing your other leg over the saddle, then put your other foot in the other stirrup."

He didn't bother to tell me which leg to use first, but I figured it had to be my left as he had me on the left side of the horse. Since I'm so tall, it really wasn't difficult to put my foot in the stirrup, pull hard, and swing myself up. And there I was, sitting pretty. I hadn't realized how high up I'd be, though. The horse was tall and it would be a long way down if I fell. But I wasn't afraid. I was thrilled!

As the horse took a couple of steps my excitement

quickly evaporated. I grabbed the saddle horn tight.

"Take the reins."

I picked up the reins that were loosely hanging over the horn.

"You need to pull them tight, but not *too* tight," Zach instructed. "When you want to go to the right you'll pull the right side, to the left, the left side."

Gingerly I pulled to the right. The horse turned and kept turning until we were going around in circles. So I pulled to the left, but the same thing happened only in the other direction.

"How do I make him go straight?" I yelled in frustration.

"Pull straight back," Zach called. He was laughing.

I didn't really mind. I must've looked pretty funny. I pulled back with both arms and Star Fire stopped going in circles. But then she started going backward. Quickly.

My heart started pounding in my chest. I knew I was in danger. The fence was close by, and if I pulled her into the fence she could hurt herself badly—and hurt me, too!

"What do I do?"

"Stop pulling so hard," Zach ordered. "Let the reins go a bit."

I let the reins go slack. Star Fire took a few more steps back, but then she stopped.

I glared at Zach. "You could have warned me!"

"Hold the reins taut, but don't pull back on them. Now give her a small kick. She'll move forward."

I did as he said. And she did move forward. One step. I gave her another tiny kick. She moved another step.

"Don't be such a sissy," Zach said. "You can give her more of a kick than that. Use both feet."

I lifted both feet out then gave her a good solid kick on both sides. She leaped forward and ran for the fence. I was so shocked I didn't know what to do, so I did the first thing I could think of: pulled back hard on the reins. She stopped dead.

I didn't.

I flew right out of the saddle, over her head, and landed flat on the ground.

The wind was knocked out of me and for a minute I couldn't breathe.

Zach leaned over me.

"You all right?"

I lifted my head. I moved my arms, then my legs. Slowly I sat up.

"You could have warned me," I repeated.

He looked at me innocently. "I don't know what you mean."

"Yes, you do. Why don't you get on her and *show* me what to do."

"No."

"No?"

"No, that's not the best way for you to learn."

I was suddenly suspicious. "Why don't you want to show me?"

"I just *said* why. Now leave it alone."

"I think I could learn better by watching you," I insisted. "And you must need to practice anyway. You'll have lots of tricks to do in the movie."

"And whose fault is that?" Zach turned on me, suddenly angry.

"What?" I was taken aback.

"If you hadn't been so darned silly, I wouldn't have to do those tricks, would I?"

"You needn't curse," I replied in my most haughty manner.

"You needn't be so darned silly," he mimicked me.

For a moment we both glared at each other and didn't say a word.

"Rosie! Did you fall off the horse?" Abe was running toward us. "I saw it from the house. Are you all right?" He raced up to the small gate, swung it open, and ran into the corral. But he didn't close the gate behind him. And before Zach could even open his mouth to tell Abe to close it, Star Fire and another horse had escaped!

Zach sprinted to the gate and closed it so none of the other horses could get out.

"We have to get them back," Zach shouted, clearly panicked.

I looked around. "It'd be better to get some of the adults to go after them, wouldn't it?" I asked.

He grabbed my arm. "If they run off for good I'll get into terrible trouble. And there's no one here but us."

"I'm coming," Abe said.

"No, you stay here and make excuses for us," I said.

"What excuses?"

"I don't know—think of something!" I said.

"They're running toward the hills," Zach said. "Hurry!"

I shrugged to Abe, turned, and ran off after Zach.

"Rosie, I don't think this is such a good idea," Abe called after me. "I should fetch Papa!"

I didn't answer. I didn't think it was a good idea either, but Zach was right. Who else would go after them if we didn't? By the time Abe found Papa the horses would be long gone.

I could still see the horses running toward the hills. They were about a half a city block away. Maybe we could catch them before they started heading into the hills. I hoped so.

Chapter 4

I HAD NEVER BEEN UP INTO THE HILLS. THERE WERE NO PATHS OR trails, and Papa refused to let us go exploring.

"All we need is for you to step on a rattlesnake," he'd say. "Or sit on a cactus."

I ran after Zach, who was amazingly fast. The horses had stopped just at the foot of the hills and were nibbling some grass. Zach was getting closer to them, slowing down so he wouldn't spook them. I could hear him talking softly to them, coaxing them to wait for him.

I slowed down too and tried to catch my breath. Zach got closer and closer to them. Just as he was close enough to reach for Star Fire's reins, a small squirrel scampered right in front of the other horse. Startled, the horse reared up and then sprinted off up the hill. Star Fire followed.

Zach cursed under his breath. He looked back at me for a second, but then, without a word, ran after them. I really didn't want to follow him—I'd never even seen a live snake and kept worrying about Papa's words. But I'd never held back because I was afraid, so I followed Zach.

I hope he knows his way around the hills, I thought, watching Zach. The fog was a worry as well. I'd noticed it earlier in the day, but then forgot all about it. Fog would often settle in the hills just behind our house but not touch the ranch at all. It was an odd phenomenon.

Zach rushed after the horses as they scrambled up a low rise at the beginning of the hills. Just over the rise was a dip, then a much higher elevation. I called to Zach, "We shouldn't go any farther than the next hill. It's too foggy."

Zach was not paying attention to me. He was running as fast as he could—once the horses went over the first rise, we'd lose sight of them. I followed, but as soon as the ground began to elevate I had to slow down. The ground in front of the hills was covered mainly in scrub, short grass, and the occasional small cactus. As soon as I began to climb, I noticed that the small shrubs grew closer together on the hillside, and it was hard to find a way around them. There were larger trees, oaks I thought, surrounded by cacti. There were pines, too, and some other trees I didn't recognize. The ground was rocky, and where there wasn't rock there was soft dirt, almost mud, from all the spring fogs and rains. I had to keep my eyes down to keep from tripping, and I soon lost sight of Zach.

When I reached the top of the small rise, though, I saw that Zach had already run down the other side and was now close to the horses.

The fog looked to me like it was getting thicker.

"Zach!" I called. "Stop!"

He either didn't hear me or didn't care to listen.

I picked my way down the side of the rise and then paused a minute. I could see Zach climbing the hill, enveloped by the fog. I started to get annoyed with him. *This fog could easily get us lost*, I thought. *Didn't I read somewhere that horses return home by themselves?*

Zach obviously didn't think they would. I supposed if he were fond of them, he wouldn't want them to get lost. Perhaps that was motivating him as much as the fear of getting in trouble. Our family had caused quite enough trouble for the troupe—I didn't want to add to it!

I sighed and began to climb. It wasn't easy. The hill was steep and slippery, and the higher I got, the thicker the fog became. Where was Zach? I couldn't even hear him near me.

"Zach? Zach!" No answer. I called again. Nothing.

About a minute later, I heard his voice off to my right.

"Over here," he called. "The horses went this way."

"I can't see you."

"Follow my voice."

Within a few minutes I found him standing in a small clearing surrounded by tall trees. He motioned for me to be quiet.

"They're that way." He pointed up and farther to the right. "I can hear them," he whispered. "If we're quiet, we'll find them."

I looked up. I could still see the sun shining faintly through the fog.

"Don't you think we should go back?" I asked. "The fog is thick, and it's getting thicker."

"Naw," he said. "It's nothing. Come on."

I followed. He stopped every minute or so to listen for the horses. I could hear the horses too, snorting and pawing the ground. But then we heard them neigh, and then heard hooves pounding. They were running again!

"That's it!" I declared. "We're never going to

catch them. Won't they find their way home?"

Zach frowned. "They *might*. But the horses don't know the area. They could get lost easy."

"Well, so could we," I stated. "I'm going back."

He kicked the dirt. "My pa is going to be pretty upset."

"He'll be *more* upset if you and I don't get back there quickly, won't he?"

"I guess you're right."

I couldn't believe he was admitting I could be right about something.

"Let's go, then," I said, not wanting to wait until he changed his mind. By now the fog had really thickened. I turned to start back, but Zach stopped me. "That ain't the way."

"Yes, it is."

"And how would you know?"

"It's the way we came," I insisted.

"Look down," Zach said. I did.

"Where are your tracks?" he asked.

I noticed they were coming from a different way altogether—in fact, from the opposite direction. "That's odd," I commented.

"No, it ain't. When the land looks the same all around, you need to follow your tracks. It's the only way out."

He led and I gladly followed. It was eerily quiet up in the hills. No birds sang. The air was chilly. And all I had on were my overalls and a long sleeved shirt. Zach was dressed the same way.

Just then, out of the quiet, came a sound. A distinct rattle.

Zach lifted his hand, motioning me to stop. "That's a rattler."

I stopped dead. For the second time that day, my heart started to pound hard. Without thinking about it, I reached forward and gripped his arm.

He laughed. "Don't worry. They don't like people. You'd have to practically step on it before it bit."

"Well," I whispered, "I suggest we go around it then." I let go of his arm, a little embarrassed.

"This way," said Zach. We took a wide circle away from the sound, and as it receded I began to breathe again.

Zach examined the ground, trying to pick up our tracks again. But he couldn't see them. Neither could I. And we could see almost nothing else for that matter. The fog, as I'd feared, had gotten thicker and thicker. I could barely see Zach right in front of me.

"I do *not* want to get lost up here," I muttered.

Zach stopped and turned to me.

"We're not gonna get lost," he said. "We're only minutes away from your house. Don't be a baby."

"Me? A baby?" I spluttered. "Oh, that's funny. I'm not *afraid*. I just don't want to get lost. It will be annoying, to say the least."

"Maybe you *should* be afraid," Zach said, his voice ominous.

"You just said I was being a baby!" I exclaimed. I was getting madder and madder at him.

He chuckled.

Now I was *boiling* mad. "You think that's funny? Well, talk about being afraid," I said. "Why wouldn't you get on Star Fire before? *You're* afraid, aren't you?"

He turned and stalked away.

"Ha!" I said. "You are!"

He stormed off so fast that I had to hurry to keep up with him.

"That's just stupid," he snapped. "I'm a trick rider. I can do anything."

"Sure you can," I said, puffing. Why was he going uphill? "You can if you get on a horse. But you're scared to, aren't you? Aren't you?"

He stopped again and turned suddenly. "You never been kicked by a horse so hard you almost died," he said, his voice flat. "Till then, maybe you'd best not say anything."

All of a sudden I felt terrible. "I'm sorry," I said. "But I could trip while walking and fall on my face. That wouldn't stop me from getting back up and walking again. Why don't you just get back on?"

"I don't know why," he said, his voice small. "I don't know. I can't explain it. I just can't do it."

"I'll help you!" I said brightly.

"You can't."

"Sure, I can."

"No," he declared, his voice angry, "you can't! Everyone's tried to help me. They've coaxed, they've bribed, they've threatened. Nothin' works. Now leave it alone!"

He turned and went back to scanning the ground for our footsteps. I followed him in silence. But the silence stretched out from a minute, to another minute, to another, and still he couldn't find our trail. I was getting cold, my feet were getting wet in my short lace-up boots, and I was getting nervous. The wilderness seemed to close in around us.

Finally I stopped. "Wait," I said.

He turned to look at me.

"Didn't you say we were only minutes away from the house?"

"Yes."

"Well, we've been walking for at least ten minutes, and we aren't even in the gully near the first small hill. Do you have any idea where we are?"

He looked at me for a moment.

"We can't be that far away from our track. I just need to keep lookin'."

"How do you even know we're going in the right direction? Why aren't we going down? Seems to me we're going up."

"We should be goin' down," he agreed reluctantly. "I was tryin' to find our footprints. Maybe we should just head down the hill, and we'll end up in the fields. Somewhere."

"I'll follow you," I said, relieved he was willing to at least listen to me. But then I heard it: neighing. And it was close by. "Listen!"

"I hear it," Zach said. "I hear it. This way."

The sound was just behind us, and it seemed very close. We turned and made our way toward the sound as quietly as we could. Then we heard the neighing again. It was definitely our horses, and it sounded like they were together. We followed the noise uphill for a bit but it was hard going; the ground was becoming more rocky, and the bushes were closer together. I brushed against a cactus with spines sticking out like a sunburst and was lucky the needles only caught on my overalls. Within the next few feet the ground started to slope downward. *What a relief,* I thought. *Maybe the horses are leading us home.* We kept going in that direction. Zach tripped once, but he was able to quickly get his footing. I just tried to keep close behind him. When we began going up again, I started to really worry.

"Zach," I whispered.

"Shh."

"Zach, listen," I insisted.

"What?"

"We shouldn't be going up again. We've gone down—why aren't we out of the hills?"

"We probably have to go up one more rise, down once more, and *then* we'll be out."

That made sense to me. "Can you still hear them?" I asked.

Zach stopped and listened. He shook his head.

"Let's wait a minute," I suggested. "Maybe they've stopped to rest."

We stood there, shivering, our breath making little puffs of smoke in front of us. We heard nothing. I looked at the sky. I couldn't see even the outline of the sun. I had no idea how long we'd been in the hills, but I thought it must be getting late.

"Zach," I said, not bothering to whisper, so my voice sounded far too loud, "we have to get home."

"I know," he said.

"I'm thirsty," I said.

"We don't want to be here overnight. No food. No water." He paused. "I've been a mite foolish. We need to get out now."

I didn't like the tone in his voice.

"You could have thought of that before dragging me up here," I complained.

"No one dragged you," he shot back. "You didn't need to come."

"Don't know why I did," I muttered. I was starting to get an uneasy feeling. I looked around. The fog was so thick I could barely see my hand if I held my arm out. "Do you have *any* idea where we are?" I asked.

"I'm not too sure," he said. "Let's head down. That's bound to get us out."

Once again we headed downhill. I almost bumped into Zach when he stopped suddenly.

"Look," he said.

We were standing on the edge of a deep ravine.

"*Oy*," I said.

"We'll have to go around it," Zach said.

That's when I knew we were lost. I think Zach knew it too. "And then what?" I asked.

"Then we'll keep headin' down. We may come out miles from where we started, but we're bound to come out."

"Are you sure?" I asked.

"Don't see why not," Zach answered with a shrug of his shoulders.

I sighed and followed him. I was thirsty, hungry, tired, and just plain grumpy. "I thought cowboys didn't get lost."

"We don't. Usually."

"But you'll admit we're lost now?"

"I wouldn't go that far," he said.

"Why not?"

"Because I still think it should be easy to get out."

Suddenly a cry ripped through the air. It was a combined scream, screech, and howl. I'd never heard anything like it. A chill shot through me as if ice were suddenly flowing in my veins.

"Mountain lion," Zach whispered.

I couldn't answer.

"We need to get down. Fast," he said.

I didn't need any coaxing. He began running beside the gully, and I was right behind him.

That is, until I fell.

Chapter 5

THE GROUND SIMPLY GAVE WAY BENEATH ME. I SLIPPED ONTO MY side, and then, with nothing to catch hold of, I rolled and kept rolling, over and over and over. I could feel the rocks and the bushes hitting me as I fell. Instinctively I put my arms over my head and face. Time seemed to slow and I felt that I would never stop tumbling. But then, suddenly and horribly, I slammed into a tree trunk. I lay there, my chest heaving, trying desperately to catch my breath, afraid to move for fear I couldn't.

Zach was calling, "Rosie! Rosie!" I knew I had to answer him, but I couldn't speak. "Rosie!"

The cry of the mountain lion tore through the air again—followed by the mournful howl of a coyote.

Wonderful, I thought. *I'm going to be dinner.* I tried to call out, but again, I couldn't. I was in such shock. Even at that moment, I knew that I needed to see how badly I was hurt. *Start slow,* I thought. Tentatively I tried to move my fingers. They moved. I wiggled my toes. They wiggled. I twisted my head. It moved. I tried to take a deep breath. A sharp pain shot across my chest. I breathed again, this time a smaller breath. That worked.

Finally I decided to try to sit up. First I raised my arms. They weren't broken. I pushed myself up until I was almost sitting with my back against the tree that had stopped me. I tried to call again.

"Zach?"

My voice came out weak and scratchy. I tried again. "Zach?" This time it was stronger.

I heard the rustling of dirt and then Zach's voice. "I'm coming." Annoying as he was, I was certainly glad to hear him coming for me.

I moved my legs. They seemed all right too. By some miracle I hadn't broken anything. "Here!" I called, this time louder.

Suddenly Zach was just in front of me. He knelt down. "Does it feel like anything is broken?" he asked.

"I don't think so," I said.

"Can you stand up?" he asked.

"I can try."

He gave me his hand and gently pulled me to my

feet. Slowly I shook out my legs and my arms, twisted around, and found that I was unhurt.

"You're bleeding," Zach said.

I looked at my hands. They were torn and ripped. "They don't hurt."

"They will," Zach said. "Right after an accident you never seem to feel the pain. But you do later. You'll be black and blue and sore all over."

"Thanks," I said. "That's something to look forward to." I looked around. We were in a deep gully that stretched as far as I could see in either direction. The top of the ravine was a good eighty feet up. I couldn't believe I had fallen that far.

"Now what?" I asked.

"Now we try to climb out of here and get home before dark," Zach answered.

I rolled my eyes. "I know *that*. But how?"

"I think we should walk along the bottom of this gully for a while. Sooner or later it'll rise up so we can get out of here."

That sounded more promising to me than trying to scramble up the steep side I'd just fallen down. "Is it starting to get dark, or am I imagining it?" I asked.

"No, it's getting dark all right," Zach said, his voice grim.

I looked up at the sky. The fog was as dense as

ever, but instead of being white, it was taking on a gray color, which meant the sun was setting. And then we heard it again: the howl of the mountain lion. This time it sounded like it was coming from right above us.

Zach grabbed my arm. He put a finger to his mouth, telling me to be quiet, and scrambled ahead. I knew that a cat like that could kill us in minutes. Just a few days before I had been studying mountain lions with Mama. Crossing that gully would be nothing for such a cat. They stalk their prey quietly and then bound out, bringing down the weak with their weight and strength. They kill by ripping out their victims' throat.

I froze on the spot. For some reason I felt that if I didn't move I'd be safer. So I stood there, barely breathing, my whole body suddenly bathed in sweat, my heart pounding. Zach had disappeared from my view, but I didn't care. I wasn't moving.

A few moments passed, then he was back.

"What's the matter with you?" he hissed. "We have to get out of here!"

I shook my head. My throat was too dry to speak.

"Come on!" he insisted.

I shook my head again.

He grabbed my wrist and pulled. I planted my feet as hard as I could. I didn't move.

"Rosie," he whispered. "Stop this."

I shook my head.

Suddenly he took my face in his two hands, locking his eyes with mine. His entire manner changed. His voice was gentle, but he held my head firmly.

"Rosie," he said softly, "you're scared."

Was this fear? I'd never felt anything like it before.

"You have to listen to me," he continued.

I noticed that his eyes were blue—a very deep blue, like the bluebells that were in bloom. The scar on his forehead stood out, a pale horseshoe on his tanned skin.

"Rosie, you need to ponder what I'm sayin' to you now. This is life or death. Do you want to live?"

I nodded.

"Then you have to come with me."

I shook my head, shaking his hands off my face. He placed them on my shoulders.

"Rosie." He was still staring into my eyes. "Can you trust me?"

I stared back. "Why should I?"

He smiled a bit, perhaps relieved that I was talking.

"Because you need to. Or you'll die. And I don't figure on leaving you. So then I'll die too."

"Just leave me," I whispered.

"No," he said simply. "That would be wrong."

Just then we heard a twig snap, not far from us. He squeezed my wrist. "Will you come?"

I nodded.

He pulled me behind him and we ran. We stumbled over rocks, and at one point I put my hand out to steady myself only to find I'd grabbed a cactus. The needles stabbed me, and the pain was awful. I didn't cry out, though.

Suddenly Zach cried, "In here!" He ducked under a tree that had fallen over and pulled me after him. I found myself crouched in a small space behind the downed tree.

"Quiet," he whispered.

Just as he spoke a huge claw swiped under the tree, ripping a strip through my pants. I pulled in my legs and screamed. Zach pulled in his legs too. The cat snarled viciously and swiped again. I didn't know I was crying until I felt the tears falling down my face.

Zach whispered in my ear. "Rosie, it can't reach us. We'll be okay. It'll go away soon." He took my hand, but I gasped in pain as the needles from the cactus that were still in my palm dug in farther.

I don't know how long the cat stayed there. It could have been five minutes; it could have been an hour. By the time we thought it might be gone, it was dark.

"We'll have to stay here till daybreak," Zach said finally. "We have no choice."

"Is it gone?"

"Don't know. It might be sitting just a few feet away, waiting for us. When it's light out, I can peek out and see. What's wrong with your hand?" he asked.

"Cactus," I said.

"Give it to me," Zach said.

I did. Slowly he picked out each of the needles. It hurt like crazy, as did everything—my whole body felt like someone had taken a hammer and pummeled me all over.

"I'm not going out there ever again," I said to him.

"We'll have to, in the morning."

"No! That cat could be anywhere, just waiting for us."

"No choice. If we stay here we'll freeze to death, or we'll die from lack of water."

"I'd rather do that then get ripped up by a

mountain lion," I countered. "Besides, everyone will come looking for us."

"And you think they'll find us in the bottom of this gully, hidden by trees so even the cat can't get to us? We have no choice. If the cat's gone, we go. Look, no use arguing now. Try to get some sleep," Zach suggested. "You can rest your head on my shoulder."

I did so without another word. I was cold, but at least Zach provided some heat. And then the strangest thing happened. A cowboy was crouching right in front of me. The same cowboy from my dreams.

"Shalom," he said.

"Shalom," I said back. "Have you come to rescue us?"

I looked to see how Zach was reacting to his presence. Zach was staring at him wide-eyed.

"I've come to talk to you about getting out of here."

"Just show us the way," I said. "We'll follow!"

"It doesn't work that way," he said. "I'm going to have to go my own way."

"Why?"

"Rules." He shrugged. By then I was pretty confused.

"Never mind, just listen. Zach is right. You need to leave in the morning."

"What about the mountain lion? Are you going to make it go away so we can go safely?" I asked.

He shook his head. "I can't, little miss. *You're* gonna have to do something."

"What?"

"Get out of here and walk to safety. Or you'll perish for sure from lack of food, and more importantly, water."

I shook my head vehemently. "I'm not moving from here!"

"You're afraid," he stated.

"Wouldn't you be?" I asked.

"Fear's a funny thing," he answered.

"How so?"

"It's your friend, it's your enemy, and it's neither of those."

"I can see how it could be your enemy," I said.

" 'The man bitten by a snake is afraid of a rope,' " he said. "That's a quote from the Talmud. Know what it means?"

I thought for a minute. "It must mean that once you've been bitten, you become afraid of anything that even *reminds* you of a snake."

The cowboy nodded. "You get crazy with fear."

"Right—it's your enemy," I stated.

"But it can also be your friend. Can you think how?"

Again I paused before I answered. "Well, when I was little, Mama put my finger on the stove for a moment. It hurt and I was afraid of it, so I didn't go near it again."

"That's a good example," he said, nodding. "And being afraid of a mountain lion is also sensible. If you walked right up to it, well, that wouldn't be very smart, would it? But you see, Rosie, fear ain't bad. It ain't good. It just is. And you can't fight it. But you can't give in to it either. Neither works."

"Well, what *does* work then?" I asked. I glanced at Zach. He was listening intently but not saying a word.

"You have to recognize the thing first. For instance, now you're saying you're afraid to leave this shelter. But staying, Rosie—that'll kill you for sure. You could freeze to death, even tonight! Your only chance here is to take a chance. You've got to walk right through your fear, or take it along with you in your pocket. It'll be there, but you'll be carrying it. It won't be ruling you.

"I gotta go now, little 'un. You can trust your friend there. He's got a good head on his shoulders. He'll need your help soon enough. But now it's his time to help you. If you need some proof, ask him about Susan."

I looked at Zach, who had a small smile on his face. When I turned back to the cowboy, he was gone.

"Rosie?"

My eyes flew open. Zach was shaking me. "It's getting light."

I was still sitting with my head on his shoulder. I looked around.

"Where is he?"

"Who?"

"The cowboy. He was just here, talking to us."

"No one's been here," Zach said gently. "You were dreamin'. I'm gonna peek out now," he said, shuffling his body around.

I was so stiff and cold I could barely move. When I did, everything hurt. I looked at my hands in the pale gray light. They were ripped and scabbed. I was so thirsty my throat hurt, and I was starving. But I was _not_ going out there. No matter what.

Zach peeked out from under the tree branch. He went farther and farther until he was completely out in the open, leaving me inside, protected. I realized that he was using himself as bait. If the cat was still there, it would pounce on him.

"It's safe, Rosie," he said. "Come out."

"No," I said. "You don't know it's safe. Come back in."

"I can't, Rosie. We need to find water. And shelter."

"We have shelter," I said stubbornly.

"Rosie, you have to trust me."

The cowboy had told me to trust him. But why should I trust the cowboy? He was just part of some strange dream. Then I remembered his words.

"Who's Susan?" I called to Zach.

Suddenly he was back in the small space with me, staring at me.

"Did my pa talk to you about her?"

"No. The cowboy in my dream did."

He seemed to go pale.

"Are you sick?" I asked.

"No. It's just that Susan was my ma."

"Your ma?"

"She died in childbirth when I was seven. Since then it's just been me and Pa."

I thought back. Had anyone mentioned her to me? I knew they hadn't. Which must mean that the cowboy was a sort of guardian angel or something.

I giggled. Zach gave me an odd look. But how many people had Jewish cowboys looking after them?

"Guess I'd better follow you," I said. "He said I should."

Zach raised an eyebrow. "You ain't a witch or anything, are you?"

I laughed. "Yes," I said, waving my hands around. "I'm going to put a curse on you!"

Zach managed a laugh too. He had a wonderful laugh. His face lit up, his eyes crinkled, his white teeth shone. "Don't curse me! Don't curse me!" he pleaded.

"I'm going to turn you into a rock!" I threatened.

"No! Not a rock. At least make me a tree, so I can sway in the wind!"

"I'll make you a cloud so you can float out of here and rescue us. Come on," Zach said. "You ready to get out of here now?"

I nodded.

"Then follow me." He wriggled out of our hiding spot again.

"Coast is clear," he called.

I took a deep breath, and then I pushed myself out of our hiding spot.

"Seems like that cat must've found another meal

somewhere," Zach said. "Hope it wasn't one of the horses. Can you walk?"

I nodded and looked around. There were tall trees everywhere. The cat could be hiding behind any of them. Slowly Zach made his way along the base of the gully. I followed, trembling with fear. I had to force myself to take every step, but I kept going. The sky was getting lighter. There was fog, but it wasn't as thick as it had been yesterday. I could see a good ten feet on either side.

"Maybe the fog'll lift with the sun," I said hopefully.

"It might," Zach agreed.

"That cowboy talked to me about being afraid," I said.

"Did he?"

"He did. He convinced me I couldn't stay put."

"Well, I'd like to thank him for that," Zach said. "I thought we were in for a big fight."

I was still nervous and looking around for the cat, but I kept walking.

"No, no fight. You're right. I was too scared to want to listen, that's all. I've never really been that scared before."

Zach began to climb up the side of the gully. I followed. Finally Zach climbed over the top. But before I could reach him, he dropped back down and put his finger over his mouth, telling me not to make a sound.

I peeked over the top of the ridge. I couldn't believe what I saw!

Chapter 6

TWO MEN LAY ON THE GROUND, WRAPPED IN SLEEPING BAGS. And tied to a tree close by were *our* two horses! I was just about to leap over the edge and thank the men when Zach quickly pulled me back down. He shook his head in warning. The horses, hearing us, whinnied. Then one of the men spoke.

"See anything?"

"Nope," said the other.

There were some rustling sounds. Maybe they were getting out of their sleeping bags?

"Can't believe these beauties just wandered into our camp," one said.

"Mulgrew is gonna give us top dollar for them, that's for certain," the other replied. "His customers love his horse meat."

I let out a gasp.

"Sure you don't hear nothing?"

"Nope. Nothing."

Zach motioned me to stay still and then whispered in my ear. "We'll wait to see if they go anywhere, then we can free the horses."

I nodded. We stayed as quiet as possible. Soon the smells of breakfast wafted toward us, causing me to nearly swoon. Biscuits . . . and some sort of meat. I hoped it wasn't horse meat!

We could barely hear anything the men said, but when they were close to the ridge, we caught some of their words.

"What a haul these horses will make. We'll wait till they're asleep tonight, and if we get them out fast enough, they won't be able to follow us, now will they? We'll be rich! Richer than rich!"

Did they mean all the horses in the corral? That was too horrible to think about. Kill all those animals? Use them as food? The whole show would be destroyed! Not to mention Papa's movies. What a disaster all around!

I turned to Zach. "We have to stop them," I whispered.

He nodded. He looked angry. _Really_ angry.

After a few minutes one of the men said, "We'll leave the horses here, go to their camp, and pretend to be interested in the show. See the setup, scout it out."

The only horses I'd seen when I peeked over the edge were the two we were chasing, which must mean the men had arrived here on foot. So we might be close to home. That thought lifted my spirits a bit. Hopefully, we weren't going to die out here.

Finally it became very quiet. Thinking the men had left, Zach climbed back up and peeked his head over the edge. He waved me forward and we scrambled into the clearing. The first thing Zach did was head for a bucket of water that had been left for the horses. He cupped his hand and drank. I did the same, but that was a big mistake. The water turned red with blood as it washed off my hands.

Zach looked around and saw a large skin near the now-cold fire. It was water. He handed it to me. I drank and drank and drank—nothing had ever tasted so good to me! After I finished Zach drank, and still almost half of the water was left, so Zach tied it to his belt. Two biscuits sat on the frying pan near the fire. I took one and gobbled it down. Zach ate the other one in two bites.

We quickly turned to the horses. Zach hurried to Star Fire to untie her. I stood watching him when suddenly I was grabbed from behind and lifted into the air.

"What the heck is going on here?" someone bellowed in my ear.

He was holding me so tight around the waist I could hardly breathe. Because of all the bruises I had, it was so painful I would have screamed—if the breath wasn't being squeezed out of me.

"Let her go!" Zach shouted, running toward me.

I took as deep a breath as I could and, despite the pain, screamed, "Run!" Then I twisted with all my strength.

Zach ran, but instead of running away, he ran straight for us. Since the fellow holding me was trying to hang on to a wriggling mass, I'm not sure he could tell what Zach was going to do. Neither could I.

What Zach did was lunge at my captor's legs, which knocked him off balance. We both toppled over. As I tried to pry myself loose, the fellow grabbed me around my shoulders. I bent my neck as far forward as I could and dug my teeth into his hand.

"Yeow!" he shrieked.

I spit to get the taste of his dirty skin out of my mouth, and scrambled away from him. Zach grabbed my arm and pulled me back down over the ridge we'd just climbed up. We were moving so fast that we practically fell down the gorge to the bottom, and then ran as fast as we could.

"On and off."

"What does that mean?"

"Whenever Pa and I are somewhere that'll take me and we're there long enough. But he needs me a lot to help with the horses and the chores, and, well, we move too much."

"Can you read?"

"I can get by."

"Write?"

"Nothin' fancy."

"Why don't you come to school with us in the morning? Mama would let you, I'm sure. She teaches us."

"If Pa could spare me."

"Do you like to learn?"

"I do. The Wild West show won't go on forever. I'd like to learn more. Maybe do somethin' else when I get older."

"Like what?"

"Don't know."

"I'll tell you what I'd like to do if you'll tell me."

He paused. "I guess I'd like to be some kind of doc. For humans *and* animals."

"I want to be a movie actress like I am now, but when I get older I'd also like to make movies. Just like Papa."

"Why?" Zach asked.

"It's fun pretending to be someone else. And it would be fun to make up stories and film them. And I'd get to boss everyone around like Papa does," I said with a grin.

"I guess it's like what we do in the Wild West show," Zach said. "We make up stories and pretend. Pa loves it, but me, well . . . I don't know, I just never loved bein' in the spotlight. But I don't have a choice. It's how we make our living."

"Tell me about some of the places you've been," I asked.

"We've been all over," Zach said. "As far north as San Francisco and east to Santa Fe, and even to Texas. Wherever we can get a booking, that's where we'll go. One year we went all the way to South Dakota. That's when the show was twice the size it is now. We went on the train. Then we got trapped there by an early snow. Took us weeks to get back down south. I've never been so cold or so miserable."

I laughed. "I know you were in Chicago, because that's where Papa met your pa, but it wasn't in the winter. You should try spending a winter *there*! But I didn't mind the cold too much. I liked it there."

"Do you like it here?"

"I *love* it here. It's like a magic fairy-tale place.

It even *smells* wonderful all the time."

"It does smell good, doesn't it? When the honey mesquite trees bloom, or the lemon trees. . . ."

"And the orange trees," I interrupted, "and grapefruit, and the flowers. So many flowers!"

"I've learned the names of all the flowers I could," Zach said.

"Really?"

"I'll prove it when we get back."

"I'm learning the names of the birds," I said. "I know, why don't I describe a flower and you see if you know the name? Then you can describe a bird and I'll see if I know the name."

"Okay," he agreed. "You first."

"It's a shrub and it has a yellow center and a lavender flower."

"That'd be a woolly aster," he answered confidently. "My turn. Its head is brown, white below, sides are striped, black-and-white mustache with streaks; it sings, 'sit-soo-see-say-soo-see.'"

"I know, I know!" I exclaimed. "That's a sage sparrow!"

Playing our new game was a good way to pass the time. Of course, neither of us would know if the other one was wrong, but we didn't care.

We were lucky Zach had taken the water. Although we were hungry, the water at least kept us feeling pretty strong. At one point we both drifted off to sleep. Finally the day started to darken. It was time to stake out the rustler's camp.

"Just try to be as quiet as you can," Zach warned me.

"I will," I promised.

He led the way back down the gully, then up the rise to the bandit's camp. They were both there, plotting their horrible crimes. We stayed well hidden behind the rise.

"You all straight then, Shorty?"

"I am. Is you?"

"I am. Let's git going. Got your gun, loaded up proper?"

"Now look here, Squinty. Just because o' that one time I forgot to load it, you don't have to keep askin' me over an' over an' over."

"Just don't want anything to go wrong. I mean, we only shoot if someone sees us, right? No point in killing anyone otherwise. Just git the law after us something awful."

"Right, only if someone gits in our way."

I could hear them readying their guns.

"The moon's jest right," one said. "Lots of light for us to find 'em."

"Or them to find us."

"Naw, they'll all be sleepin' like little bitty babies."

"I sure hope so. Let's get outta here."

"Right behind you."

Zach nodded to me, then pulled himself up over the rise so he could follow them. I fervently hoped that he would follow quietly enough not to get caught.

As I waited all the sounds of the wild became far too loud for comfort. A coyote howled. I heard an owl screech. I wondered what kind of snakes and spiders were crawling around me. Then I reminded myself that there was no point dwelling on these things, and to occupy my mind I tried to recite a poem Mama had made me memorize a few days earlier.

Tyger! Tyger! burning bright
In the forests of the night,
What immortal hand or eye
Could frame thy fearful symmetry?

In what distant deeps or skies
Burnt the fire of thine eyes?

I stopped. This wasn't helping! I supposed Mama hadn't realized I'd be facing a big cat myself.

Suddenly I heard Zach's voice. "Rosie?"

I practically leaped up over the rise.

He stood there, hands on hips, a small grin on his face. "I know how to get back to the ranch."

I was so relieved, both that he was back safe and that he knew the way out, that I almost hugged him.

"Now we just have to ride the horses out," I said.

I could see his troubled face clear as day in the light of the full moon. Would he be able to? I wasn't sure. And I could tell he wasn't either.

Chapter 7

ZACH APPROACHED THE TWO HORSES. STAR FIRE WHINNIED AND nuzzled him.

"You are a very bad girl," he scolded her. "No use trying to make up with me now." He patted the other horse as well. "This is Texas," he said to me. "We bought him there, and he has a spirit like the state; he loves open spaces and running as fast as he can."

He looked around, then made a clucking noise with his tongue. "Only one saddle."

"That's not good," I said. "What should we do?"

"I'll saddle Star Fire for you," Zach said. "I'll have to ride Texas bareback."

"Can you?"

"I'm a trick rider," he answered. "I can ride any way, any how."

"But *will* you?"

He didn't answer, but he started to saddle Star Fire.

"I can run pretty fast," he said. "Maybe I can tie a rope around Texas and we'll follow you, me running behind you and Star Fire."

"First of all," I said, "I'll be lucky to stay on Star Fire at all. Secondly, I'll need to follow you—and so will she. You know that. So if you aren't going to ride, there's no point in my riding either."

"Good, then," he said, "that's what we'll do. We'll lead the horses out."

"And we'll be too late."

"Not if we run."

"You know that's not true. The bandits are well ahead of us. And they're bigger than us! They can move faster. Also they aren't pulling horses behind them. If we want to save the horses and my Papa's movie, we'll have to ride—as fast as the horses can go." I paused. "You know I'm right. Look, just don't think about it. Think about saving the horses, not about you. Let's just go!"

He finished cinching the saddle and helped me up. My stomach was full of butterflies. Riding in the night, in the wilderness, wasn't my idea of a beginner's lesson. But we had to do it.

Zach stared for a moment at Texas. He patted the horse and said something that I couldn't hear. Then Zach took a deep breath. Grabbing a handful of Texas's mane, he pulled himself up in one grace-ful movement. It was a thing of beauty to see. Texas skittered a bit, and Zach patted him, speaking softly. I couldn't see his face, but I could see the ten-sion in his shoulders and his back.

He turned to me. "Ready?"

"Ready as I'll ever be."

Without another word he urged Texas forward. He went in quite the opposite direction I thought we'd go to get out. But I didn't have time to question him. I needed to focus on holding on to Star Fire, who immediately started jarring me up and down. She wasn't galloping, so I had to assume this was what was called trotting. My bottom slammed down onto the saddle every couple of seconds, my teeth rattled in my mouth, and every bruise I had gotten from rolling down the gully the day before screamed in pain. Star Fire picked her way up a rise, following Texas.

I was beginning to think my head would bounce right off when we crossed the rise of the hill and began going down. The jarring only became worse as Star Fire trotted down the hill at a pace I felt was very unsafe. Still, what choice did we have? We needed to get home. Fast.

"This is as far as I followed them," Zach called

back. "But I think if we keep going in this direction, we should be all right."

I hoped his assumption was correct. And I hoped I could stay on the horse. An owl screeched. Star Fire gave a little jump.

"Pat her," Zach called back. "Try to keep her calm."

I tried, even though *I* wasn't calm at all. In fact, I kept imagining mountain lions waiting for us behind every tree, ready to leap. As I thought about this I managed to pat Star Fire and tell her that we were safe, and that nothing was going to hurt us.

"When we reach the camp," Zach called back to me, "I'll have to get to the bell we ring for emergencies."

"Are you all right?" I called to him.

"I'm on a horse," he replied. "That's somethin', I guess."

After that all conversation stopped, as we needed all our energy for the difficult ride. I held on for dear life. For some reason a funny idea occurred to me. I thought back to my life in New York such a short time ago—a year and a half—and how I never, *never* could have imagined myself in this situation. Even if my neighbor Mrs. Yaffeh, who could see the future, had said, "Rosie, I see you riding a horse through the dark in the wilds of California," I would have said, "Mrs. Yaffeh, this time you are *meshugge*!" I giggled out loud. Because my teeth were chattering in my head, the sound came out rather oddly.

"What's that?" Zach called to me.

"Nothing. Sorry!"

We had reached the bottom of one hill and the horses began climbing up another. They were strong, and although they needed to slow down on the way up to pick their way around the cacti and rocks, they still made far better time than we could have on foot. It was a steep climb. Because Zach didn't have a saddle he had to fall forward onto Texas's neck and hang on as his horse climbed up.

And then, at the top of the rise, we saw Hollywood, all lit up, right beneath us! There was a path that led almost straight down, over a smaller rise, and then into the city. I assumed our ranch was just over to the right; I could see a few small fires there that looked like the camp. I thought about poor Mama and Papa and how worried they must be. They would have worried even more had they known we'd met bandits and a mountain lion!

"Let's hurry," Zach said, and he urged his horse forward. The horses must have smelled home because they picked up the pace. They trotted down the hill, sidestepping trees and brush, then trotted up and down small hills until we were on flat ground.

Suddenly they flew into a gallop. As Star Fire's stride grew long, it was easier to sit in the saddle. I held on, bending over her neck for balance. The air whipped my hair out of my face, and all I could feel was the power of the beautiful creature carrying me home. It was one of the most thrilling moments of my life.

The horses headed straight for the corral, but we needed to get to the camp first. Zach couldn't steer his horse in any subtle way, and I realized that since I was the one with the reins, I needed to lead. I didn't know where the bell was, but I knew we needed to go around the corral, so I kicked Star Fire for some extra speed and pulled her to the right just as Zach had taught me. She moved as if I'd been riding her for years. We overtook Zach, and Texas followed us.

As we rode into camp, people were already running toward us. They must have heard the horses' hooves. As I slowed Star Fire, Zach leaped off his horse. He grabbed the hammer and struck the bell hard. Then again.

"Bandits!" he called. "Look to the horses!"

In no time, flares were lit from the fire. The men grabbed their guns and raced for the corral. I sat on Star Fire, unsure how to dismount. Zach didn't forget about me, though. He hurried over and lifted me down. We paused a minute, his hands still around my waist.

"Thank you," I said, gazing into his eyes.

He smiled. And did he blush? "You're welcome," he answered, letting go of me and turning to Star Fire. He tied her to a post, put a rope around Texas, and tied him up too. "After all this, best if they don't run off again, don't you think?" he said.

I laughed. "I *do* think."

Just then I heard Papa's voice booming, "What is it?"

"Papa," I screamed, "it's me. I'm back!"

He ran out of the darkness and swept me up in his arms. "Rosie!" He covered me with kisses. "Rosie, we've been worried to death. Don't move, I'm going to get your mama."

"Papa, there are bandits!"

"Then you'd better run back to the house. Tell Mama and the boys to stay there until it's safe."

I looked at Zach.

"I'm going to help the others," he told us.

"You leave that to us, Zach," Papa said firmly.

"You go with Rosie. Your pa hasn't taken a bite to eat since you two ran off." He shook his head. "I can't imagine what you were thinking."

Just then we heard shouts, and then shots from the corral. "Go!" he ordered us.

Zach and I ran to the house and raced onto the porch just as Abe and Joe ran out of the house to see what was happening.

"Rosie!" Abe exclaimed. He actually hugged me! And so did Joe.

"Mama!" screamed Abe.

At that moment Mama burst out of the door just behind the boys. She stopped dead when she saw me, then swooned. Abe and I caught her and helped her back inside. We carefully set her on a chair in the front parlor.

"Go get her some water," I ordered Abe. "You go too," I said to Joe. "And please get me and Zach something to drink."

I patted Mama's cheeks gently. Slowly, she opened her eyes. "Rosie? Is that really you?"

"Yes, Mama."

"I thought you were dead! We searched all day for you."

Abe came back with two glasses of water. He gave one to me and helped Mama sip the other one. Joe brought Zach a glass of water too. Zach drank it in one big gulp, then asked where his pa was.

"In the sitting room, where he was when you left," Joe said.

Zach hurried to see his pa. Meanwhile, there was a terrible ruckus outside. Shots were fired, horses were neighing, and men were shouting and screaming.

"What on Earth is going on?" Mama asked.

"Yes, what?" Abe repeated.

"Bandits!" I said dramatically.

"Bandits?" Mama looked very alarmed. "Rosie, where have you *been*?"

"We got lost trying to find the horses, Mama. And then we came upon these robbers. They'd captured the horses and were planning to come here and steal the rest. And they were going to sell them for *horsemeat*!"

"But are you all right, Rosie?" Mama asked. "You aren't hurt?" She noticed my hands. "Rosie, your hands! Oh, my. Where's Papa? He's not *out* there, is he? Did I hear *guns*?" The color drained from her face and she looked like she might faint again.

"Don't worry, Mama, those Wild West cowboys can shoot better than anyone."

The door slammed.

"That must be Papa," I said. I ran out of the parlor to greet him. But it wasn't him. It was the bandits! And they had guns out—pointed straight at me.

"You!" said one of them. He was short and stocky with thick black hair, black eyes, and a rough face with a scar that reached from his eye to his chin. He must have been the one called Shorty.

The other one was tall and thin. His hat was pulled low over his narrow eyes, but he still managed to give me a menacing look.

"She's the one that bit me," the taller one said. His eyes narrowed even further.

I couldn't let him near Mama and the boys. I had to think fast. Before I could do anything, Joe ran out of the room into the hallway calling, "Papa!" When he saw the two men, though, he stopped dead.

"Get goin'," Shorty said to me. "Move."

"Where?" I managed to say.

"In there," he said, pointing to the parlor.

"No," I objected, "the kitchen's better. You must be hungry."

I wanted to keep them away from Mama.

"In there," the other insisted.

"You'd best listen to Squinty," Shorty said. "He doesn't like it when he gets bit. Not a bit." He laughed at his own joke.

They pushed us into the room. Mama leaped from her chair when she saw them. She took a deep breath and drew herself up so fast you never would have known she'd almost fainted a few minutes ago. "What is the meaning of this?"

Mama motioned me, Abe, and Joe over, then pushed us behind her.

"Well, ma'am, I'll tell you the meaning. You ever heard of a hostage?"

"I think so," she replied.

"Well, consider yourself and your kids just that. My partner and me, we wanna git out of here. *With* the horses. And it didn't much look like we would. Till now that is. Now I'm feeling a whole lot better."

Just then I saw Zach standing at the entrance to the parlor. He looked shocked.

"Run!" I screamed.

Zach didn't need to be told twice. He ran, and the door slammed behind him. He'd gone for help. But what would they do? If Papa didn't give them what they wanted, we'd be dead before anyone could get to us.

"That's good," Squinty said. "He'll go git 'em, and then we'll see if any of you is gonna live beyond tonight."

Mama spoke quietly. "No one is going to get hurt here, sir. You'll get what you want and then you'll leave us in peace."

"Well," said Shorty, "that sounds good to me."

Chapter 8

"YOU ALL GIT OVER THERE ON THAT SETTEE WHERE I CAN SEE you," Shorty ordered. He pulled the curtains back with his gun and peered outside. I could hear shouts and see the torches moving toward us.

Shorty looked us over. "You," he said, pointing to Joe.

"Yes?" Joe said.

"You can tell them what we want."

Joe stood up. Mama looked a little relieved. At least Joe would get out safely.

"Tell them we want all the horses. And they should tie them together so we can take them out easy. And you all need to stay behind." He thought. "We'll take the hand biter with us and let her go when we're safe away."

"No!" Mama exclaimed.

"You ain't got no say in this," Squinty commented.

"Take me instead," Mama insisted.

"Naw, she's got enough spunk she won't faint away or nothin'. We'll take her."

I didn't know whether to be flattered or scared. I decided to be flattered. They didn't scare me! Well, not half as much as the mountain lion. But when I thought about being let out there in the wild, just me and the mountain lion and the coyotes, my blood ran cold.

"We'll promise not to go after you," Mama said. "No one will agree to let you take her, though."

"Well, I guess they won't have much choice, will they?" Squinty said.

"You go tell 'em what we want," Shorty said to Joe.

Joe looked at Mama. She nodded to him. Slowly he started out of the room.

"Get a move on!" Shorty ordered.

Joe sprinted the rest of the way.

We waited in silence for a few moments. Then we heard Papa's loud voice.

"We're willing to talk," he shouted from outside. "One of you, come out."

Shorty motioned to Abe. "You go to the door and tell them that one of them can come in. We ain't going out there. And if you run off I'll jest shoot this girl here. She your sister?"

"She *is* my sister," Abe answered, "and you'd better not hurt her!"

"Or you'll do what?" Squinty laughed.

"You'll find out," Abe declared.

"Just get out there," Shorty ordered.

Abe left the room, went to the door, and shouted, "They say one of you can come in." Then he returned to the parlor.

Shorty left the room to stand by the door and make sure only one person came in. In a minute Papa came into the room. He looked at us.

"Are you all right?" he asked. He hurried over to Mama.

"We're fine," she assured him.

Papa turned to the bandits. "We agree to everything, but you can't take Rosie. She'd never survive out there when you let her go. The young boy that was with her, Zach, he'll go with you. He's volunteered."

"No, Papa!" I exclaimed.

"Rosie." Papa glared at me so hard he scared me. "You aren't to get involved. Be quiet."

Papa had never used a tone like that with me before. I didn't dare say another word.

"It'll take us a while to get the horses ready for you," Papa said.

"Here's the thing," Shorty said. "We'll take the boy. And he can make sure the girl gets out. They'll both go."

Papa opened his mouth to object, but before he could speak Squinty said, "There's nothin' more to say. We've made up our minds. This way no one gits hurt."

"You don't know that," Papa objected. "Those two children got lost last time. They could easily be hurt."

"But," said Shorty, "at least they won't be dead. Right now we ain't got nothin' to lose. You'll shoot us dead if we just leave with no hostage. And so we may as well shoot you all right now." He cocked his gun and pointed it straight at me.

"No!" Papa said. "You're right. You say the way it'll be. I'll go tell the others and we'll get everything ready. We'll send Zach in to get you."

He gave Mama a kiss and whispered something to her. Then he did the same to Abe. Then me. "Be ready for anything, Rosie," he whispered in my ear.

I didn't know what that meant, but I hoped it meant he had a plan. Maybe he was just encouraging me to be ready when we left—to try to escape. That made the most sense. Much as I was sorry that

Zach would be in danger, I was relieved to know he'd be with me. And I was awfully impressed that he had volunteered to put himself in danger for me. It made me feel all funny inside.

As Papa left, Squinty turned to Mama. "We could sure use a drink. You got any liquor?"

"No," Mama said. She was lying. We had wine. But drunk bandits would be a very bad thing. "Let me get you some fresh lemonade. And some cake I just made."

Shorty nodded. "You go help her," he said to me. "And if you decide to run, well, your brother here, he'll pay the price."

Mama motioned me to follow her. We hurried into the kitchen where she stopped and drew me into her arms for a long hug. "Rosie," she said, "we're in quite a pickle."

"I know, Mama."

"Now put that lemonade on the table and fetch me the sugar." She began foraging in the cupboards for something.

"What are you looking for, Mama?" I asked.

"Add a couple of lemons to the lemonade," she ordered. "And two tablespoons extra sugar."

I was puzzled, but I started to do as she'd ordered.

"Here it is!" she declared. She hurried over to the table with a small vial in her hand. I recognized it. Valerian root. She used it to help us sleep when we were ill. She dumped the entire vial into the pitcher of lemonade.

"Mama," I said, my voice full of admiration, "you are so clever!"

"It won't knock them out completely, Rosie," she warned me. "But it should slow them down. You must watch for an opportunity to escape before you end up so far away that you'll never find your way home."

"I will, Mama," I promised.

"Now cut the cake. And take some of those cookies, too." She gave me a kiss. "We'll come through this, Rosie. Let's get back before they become suspicious."

I filled a plate with cake and cookies and put two glasses on a tray. I carried the sweets back to the parlor, and Mama brought the pitcher of lemonade.

When we returned to the parlor Mama poured both men their lemonade. They took it and drank. Shorty loved it and drank all of his, but Squinty wrinkled his nose. "Too sour," he said, and put the glass down after one gulp.

"I can sweeten it for you," I offered.

"Nah. Never liked lemonade much."

"It's good for ya," Shorty lectured him. "Ma always told me to drink up my lemonade."

"Well, you ain't my ma," Squinty replied.

"I'll sweeten it up," I said again.

"Oh, all right," Squinty agreed.

I hurried to the kitchen with his glass and added a full spoon of sugar. When I took it back he gulped down about half the glass, but put the rest down. "Just get me some water," he demanded.

When I returned to the kitchen, I found Zach coming in from the sitting room.

"Zach!"

"You all right, Rosie?"

"Yes. But you shouldn't have volunteered to do this. You could get hurt. And your pa . . . well, it would be hard on him."

"I couldn't leave you out there alone," he said, and he seemed to blush a bit as he said it.

I was so struck by his words I didn't know how to answer. I was overwhelmed and a little embarrassed and very, very thankful. In the end all I could manage to say was, "Thank you."

"Listen," he said, but Squinty interrupted him with a shout.

"Where's my water?"

"When I yell drop, you get to the floor," Zach said as I poured the water. "Tell your ma and brother the same."

Squinty was standing at the kitchen door.

"Where'd you come from?" he asked suspiciously.

"Just came in the back way," Zach said. "I was thirsty."

I handed Zach the water I'd just poured. As he drank it I poured another. "Here's your water," I said quickly to Squinty.

"You two get back there," he said, waving his gun. "Are we all set to go then, boy?"

"Yep, we are," Zach said. We returned to the parlor.

"They're gonna ring the bell when they're ready," Zach said. "Then you can go out the front door. The horses will be tied together for you. Everyone will be back in the camp, so you don't have to worry about an ambush."

"That's good," Shorty said, "because if anyone were to do that, well, you and little Rosie here would be the first to go."

I thought he was starting to talk a little slower. In fact, he slumped into a chair. "Give me some more of that drink," he ordered Mama. "I feel mighty parched."

Mama poured him more lemonade. Unfortunately, Squinty was now drinking his plain water instead.

I needed to find a way to tell Zach to be ready to run. But then, knowing Zach, he'd be ready for anything.

Mama motioned me over to her and I sat down beside her on the settee.

"Rosie," she said in a low voice, "I just want you to know that you *are* going to come through this."

"I know, Mama," I said, finding myself reassuring her. "You mustn't worry. Zach got us out of there once, and he'll do it again. Oh," I said, remembering, "he says be ready to drop when he yells."

"Rosie, I know you trust Zach. But you can trust yourself, too. You are smart and fast. Just listen to your instincts."

"Don't I always?" I managed a smile.

She managed one back. "Of course you do."

Just then, the bell rang. I grasped Mama's hand. She kissed me on the forehead. Then I stood up, took a deep breath, and got myself ready for what might come next.

Shorty got out of his chair and motioned for me and Zach to come over to him. He was facing away from the foyer. Squinty was looking out the window.

And that's when I saw him. The King. He stood holding himself up with his crutch under his left arm. In his right arm was a gun. Mama and Abe saw him too. Zach said, quietly so as not to startle the bandits, "Drop."

I took hold of Mama and Abe and pulled them hard to the floor before they really understood what was happening. Zach dropped too. And Billy shot. The gun flew out of Shorty's hand, and a second after that Squinty's gun was shot away too!

Zach raced over and grabbed both guns. As he did this, the front door burst open and Bella ran in shooting. Both men screamed as gunshots flew over their heads. The rest of the troupe flooded in behind Bella. They picked up the two bandits and carried them off. Within seconds it was all over.

Papa burst into the room, ran over to us and smothered us in kisses and hugs. Zach helped his pa into a chair. The King smiled. "Foolish of them to try to rob a crowd of sharpshooters." Everyone burst out laughing.

Was it all over? Truly?

One of the men came in. "Ready to drive them varmints in to the police station?" he asked Papa.

"I'm ready, all right," Papa said. He gave us each an extra kiss and then hurried off.

Zach and I looked out the door to be sure the two bandits were actually gone. Sure enough, they were in the back of Papa's truck, howling like babies. I suppose nearly getting shot must be scary. I was just glad I hadn't had to find out myself. We watched Papa drive off and then went back to the parlor.

"May I have some of the lemonade?" Zach asked. "I'm sure thirsty."

Mama smiled. "I'll make a fresh batch. Rosie, want to help me?"

"Yes, Mama," I said. "I think it's best we pour this out."

"Why?" asked the King.

"Because Mama put valerian root in it," I said proudly.

He nodded in admiration. "Well, that surely made my job easier. I wondered why they didn't turn and shoot back."

"Not only will I make lemonade," Mama said, "but I suspect we have two very hungry youngsters here."

"That's for sure," Zach said.

I realized just then how hungry I was. I almost felt faint from it.

We went into the kitchen, and soon the table was covered with cold meat, boiled potatoes, pickles, bread, butter, and some fresh lemonade. Zach helped his pa in, and he sat with us, his leg raised on a second chair. Joe and Abe sat down too.

"Now," Mama said, "I want to hear everything. Right from the beginning."

But I was too hungry to talk. So was Zach. And by the time we had stuffed ourselves, I suddenly felt like I couldn't stay awake for one more minute.

"Abe," Mama said, "help me draw baths for these two. Rosie, you first. You need a good wash before bed. And I need to put some salve on those hands."

The bathtub was in a separate room at the back, with the toilet. This was a special thing Mama had added to the house before we moved in. And it was the best part, as far as I was concerned.

Abe ran the water for me and soon I sank into a tub full of heat. It was heaven. Mama helped me scrub my hair. We discovered that a few bugs had taken up residence on my head, but soon they were floating around in the water. It hurt when my hands were washed. When I was dry and in my nightdress

Mama put salve on my hands and then covered them with gloves. As Mama walked me to my room, she assured me that Abe would help Zach get cleaned up. She tucked me into bed like she had when I was younger.

"Rosie, Rosie," she said, shaking her head. "There's never a dull moment with you around."

I grinned. "That's true, Mama."

She smiled and gave me a kiss. "Sleep tight."

But her voice floated to me from far away as I drifted off into dreams.

Chapter 9

THE BLACK PHOEBE WAS SINGING OUTSIDE MY WINDOW. I WENT to look, and much to my surprise, the Jewish cowboy was sitting in the tree with the bird.

"Shalom!" He grinned at me.

"Shalom!" I smiled back.

"You did very well out there, helping your friend."

"I tried," I said modestly.

"Now it'll be his turn again. Just remember what I said. You put that fear in your pocket and take it with you."

"With me where?"

"Time to wake up now, Rosie."

Slowly I opened my eyes. The black phoebe was singing outside the window. I leaped out of bed and ran to look. No cowboy.

I took a deep breath and stretched. As usual, the smell of flowers was sweet. I put on my dressing gown and padded to the kitchen, my stomach rumbling with hunger. Just as I reached the kitchen door, which was partially ajar, I heard Mama saying, "What on Earth are we going to do?"

"I don't know, dear," Papa answered. "Perhaps you can get a job in a factory for a while. I'll try to see if any of the other movie companies would hire me. . . ."

"And you're sure there's no way but to sell?"

"Not unless you can tell me how we can make a hit movie in a day."

I walked into the room.

"Rosie!" Papa said. He gave me a big kiss.

"How are you, darling?" Mama asked.

"I feel wonderful," I said, peeling the gloves off. I checked my hands. "And look, Mama, my hands are much better."

"That's good, *pitsele.* Sit down. I'll get you some breakfast."

"What were you talking about just now?" I asked as I sat down. "I thought you were going to build a set and film a Western."

Papa sighed. "We haven't been able to find wood quickly enough for a set. We can get some sent to us, but it'll arrive in a few weeks. In the meantime, there's too much money going out and not enough coming in. It cost me for the loan, it cost me to hire the Wild West show. I'd need to send at least two or three films to Chicago and New York this week to make enough money to pay our bills."

"Why don't we do the same kind of films we were doing before?" I asked.

Papa shook his head. "People are demanding new stories, Rosie. The Westerns are perfect, but we don't have any more time to develop them. I'm afraid I didn't think things through very well when I hired the Wild West show. It's too expensive."

"But can't you film something without building a set, Papa?" I asked.

"Yes, Rosie, but we spent lots of time looking for you, and I haven't had a chance to think up a story. If we don't film today, it'll be too late. Our bills are due next week. We have to send off a film tomorrow!"

"Did Mama tell you all about my adventure with Zach yesterday and the day before, Papa?"

"Yes," he said. He patted my head. "I'm glad nothing scares you, Rosie. It would have been much worse for you if you'd been frightened. I consoled myself when you were lost that though you might be in danger, at least you weren't afraid."

If only he knew! Still, I smiled and said, "You

know me, Papa. Nothing scares me." Then I paused before I made my suggestion. "But why don't you make a film of what happened to me and Zach? It could be a serial in three parts. First we'd get lost and be chased by the mountain lion. That part could end with us finding the hiding place. And then the second film could be of us finding the bandits and almost getting caught. And in the third film we'd be held hostage."

Papa stared at me for a moment. "Rosie," he declared, "that's a wonderful idea! We won't need a set—we can go up into the hills to film. Two of the Wild West cowboys can play the bandits. And you and Zach can play yourselves!"

"Who will play the mountain lion?" Mama joked.

"I'll film one at the fair in town," Papa said, so excited he could barely sit still. "I can make it look like it's after you even though it won't be."

My heart sank a little. I hadn't thought that I'd have to go back into the hills, with all the dangers there. But I couldn't tell Papa I didn't want to do it. It was my idea, after all. And it would save his business.

"Zach is out at the corral, Rosie. Run and ask him if he'll do it. I'm going to go to town to see if I can film their mountain lion. I'll be back after lunch, and we'll start shooting right away. I can send the film off tomorrow morning, and then we can shoot the second one. We'll do each film as a two-reeler. Twenty minutes each! Once they are done we can even show them together. All three together will run an hour. This is wonderful!" Papa ran off without another word, and within minutes I heard the truck leaving.

"Here, Rosie," Mama said, "you'd better eat." She put some porridge in front of me, with a thick slice of bread and strawberry preserve. I slathered the preserve on the bread and gobbled it down.

"Mama, my overalls are filthy," I said. "What can I wear?"

"Abe's trousers will be too short on you," Mama said. "Tell you what, I'll wash your overalls and hang them in the sun. Hopefully they'll dry by the time Papa gets back."

"Thanks, Mama," I said. "I'm going to find Zach."

I hurried to my room, put on my skirt and a blouse, and ran out of the house. The camp was bustling with activity. Papa must have already gotten everyone busy for the filming that afternoon, although not too many of the members of the troupe would be needed yet. Most would only be used in part three.

I got to the corral and saw Zach throwing a saddle on Star Fire. He saw me and waved.

"Come for your lesson?"

"I can't," I said, "my overalls are being washed. But I'd like to learn how to put on the saddle." I paused. "And then you could ride her and show me."

He gave me a small smile. "I know what you're doing."

"Will it work?"

"It might. Come over here and I'll take you through this." He took the saddle off and put it on the ground. "First put it on her back." I reached down to lift it up and was shocked at how heavy it was. I could barely get it off the ground.

"How much does it weigh?" I asked.

"Almost thirty pounds," he answered. "And this is a plain one. Pa's fancy one, that's a good forty pounds."

"Well, how on Earth am I going to get it on her?" I asked.

He grinned. "You aren't. Not until you start to build up some more arm strength." He lifted the saddle and swung it up. Then he showed me how to cinch it, adjust the stirrups, and put on the bit and the bridle. He seemed nervous while saddling, calmer when he was done.

"Did you get kicked when you were saddling?" I asked when Star Fire was ready.

"No," he answered. "But you can, easy. Or get bit."

"So, how . . . ?" I pressed.

"I was showing off. You know that trick—grabbing a scarf from the ground? I dipped down on one side of the horse, then tried to swing *under* the horse and back on top on the other side. I didn't quite make it."

"That sounds like a daring feat," I said.

"You don't think it sounds foolish?"

"No," I said. "Not at all."

"You're a funny girl," he said.

"I suppose. Things don't scare me."

He raised his eyebrows.

"Well, except mountain lions. Don't know why I was so terrified, though."

"They usually aren't anything to worry about," he said. "Mountain lions are pretty cowardly, really."

"Well, that one wasn't."

"She must've had cubs nearby. And maybe hunting had been bad that day. You know, all animals are different. You can even get some horses with nasty natures."

By now he'd finished getting Star Fire ready. "So," I said, "are you going to get on her?"

"Yep," he answered. "I'm gonna."

"So, do it," I prodded him.

"I'm gonna."

"Zach," I reminded him, "you did it yesterday. The more you do it, the easier it'll get."

Grimacing slightly, he put his foot in the stirrup and swung up.

"There you go!" I said, very pleased. As he started to walk her I called up to him, "How would you like to be in Papa's newest film?"

"Me?"

"Papa wants to film the story of what happened to the two of us."

"Why'd you wait till now to ask?"

"I wanted to see if you could get up on Star Fire. If you couldn't, well, there'd be no point. But there you are!"

He grinned down at me. "It feels good. Wait, what about you? Are you ready to go back up there? To mountain lion country?"

"No." I paused. "But I have no choice. If I don't do it, Papa's whole business will fail."

"Don't worry," Zach said. "I'll help you through it."

"I know you will," I said, and smiled.

Zach took Star Fire out of the corral and rode her around. Watching him was like being in a nickelodeon and watching a movie. It was magic—as if he and the horse were one. I forgot all about the time until I heard Papa's horn beeping.

Zach rode back to the corral and said he was going to feed and water Star Fire. I hurried back to the house.

"Rosie, look what I've bought you!" Papa was beaming as he got out of the truck pulling a package behind him. I followed him into the house. One by one, and with much dramatic flair, he pulled the items out of the bags. First came a blue denim skirt, but it was split down the middle, so really, it was a pair of very wide-legged pants. It had a leather fringe on the bottom and strip of leather fringe just above that. Next came a bright red blouse with an open collar, with a black neckerchief to go around it.

I gasped. "Papa! They're wonderful!"

"Wait!" he said. "There's more."

He pulled out soft brown leather boots that looked like they would lace up well over my knees.

"Oh, Papa!" I exclaimed.

Joe and Abe had heard Papa come in, and they raced in from the back porch where they'd been studying.

"Rosie gets all that?" Abe exclaimed. "Not fair!"

"One more thing," Papa said. With a flourish he pulled the most magnificent cowgirl hat from a large brown bag.

I shrieked with delight.

"Go try it on, Rosie," Papa said with a smile.

As I grabbed up my treasures, Papa said to Abe, "Don't worry. When we film the bank robbery, you'll get a wonderful costume."

"When will that be?" Abe said grumpily.

"In a couple of weeks, if all goes well with the set," Papa replied.

"Fine," Abe said. "If you promise."

"I promise," Papa said. "Besides, you'll need that time to learn to ride."

"Oh, I suppose," Abe conceded grudgingly.

I hurried off to change. When I made my grand entrance into the kitchen, Mama clasped her hands. "Rosie, you look like a real cowgirl."

"Thanks, Mama." I turned to Papa. "What about Zach? Does he get a costume?"

"He has one from the show," Papa said.

"Now, no one is going anywhere," Mama said,

"until you've eaten. Abe, run and get Zach. He'll need a good meal too."

Soon Abe returned with Zach. Mr. King was also invited to lunch, and we all had a merry time as he told us wonderfully exciting stories about their show and their tours.

As he spoke I suddenly had a wonderful idea. I waited impatiently for a chance to speak, and when there was finally a lull in the conversation, I made my suggestion.

"Papa, wouldn't it be wonderful if someone like Mr. King could help you make your Westerns? He knows everything about riding and stunts, and he knows a bit about the theater side, too."

For a moment no one spoke. I held my breath. What if Papa thought it was a bad idea? He'd be embarrassed to say that to Mr. King in front of everyone. Had I spoken out of turn?

But Papa smacked the table with his hand and turned to Cowboy King. "You know, that's a magnificent idea! What do you say, sir? You could settle down here with us and be our stage manager and stunt coordinator."

Cowboy King looked at Zach. Zach nodded. Cowboy King nodded too, and turned back to Papa. "Why, I guess that would be a fine offer," he answered. "Just fine. It means we'll be staying on here for a while, son," Mr. King said to Zach. "If that's all right with you."

Zach grinned. "Sounds good, as long as Mrs. Lake will invite us to eat with her every once in a while. She cooks a lot better than you do, Pa. No offense."

"None taken, Zach," Mr. King said.

I stole a glance at Zach and could see that he was pleased. So was I. It would be exciting working in films together. And he'd be able to study with us as well.

After lunch Zach and I went to the corral to begin reliving our experiences in front of the camera. Papa had already set up the camera outside the corral. The members of the show were gathered behind him, ready to watch.

"Don't worry, Rosie," Zach said. "No big cat is really going to come after us this time. There are far too many people."

"Doing it this way *is* easier, isn't it?" I asked.

Zach nodded. "Easier, yes. But I'll never forget our adventure."

"Neither will I," I said.

"Ready, Rosie? Ready, Zach?" Papa asked, as he began to roll the camera. "Go to the corral and start to saddle the horses. Abe, you get ready to come in, and leave the gate open behind you."

Then Papa shouted, "All right, everyone! Action!"

WHEN YOU GO TO SEE A MOVIE YOU ARE DRAWN INTO THE world on the screen. For a few hours you suspend your disbelief and sink into a world of make-believe. But in order for the movie to be as real as it is, there are many different things going on behind the scenes. There are actors who work very hard at developing their characters; there are directors who work very hard at creating a wonderful story; there are writers who work very hard at writing something exciting and magical; there are set designers, art directors, props people, makeup artists, and others.

How movies developed from the very earliest silent pictures to the amazing blockbusters of today is a fascinating story. The story I tell in this book is only the tip of the iceberg, with the setting of the tale at the very beginning of the film industry—a time before the big studios, when independent producers had no road map, had no path to follow, and were the trailblazers.

When writing a historical novel I try to develop an exciting story that is based on historical fact. In order to do that the first thing I must do is research. When my husband and I traveled to California in the winter of 2003, the main reason, aside from escaping the cruel winters of Winnipeg, was to research *Rosie in Los Angeles*. Shortly after we arrived, we were very fortunate to notice that the Autry Museum of Western Heritage was advertising an exhibit titled "Jewish Life in the American West." We hurried from our temporary home in the desert into Los Angeles to visit the museum. The exhibit was both fascinating and informative. We saw pictures of Jewish cowboys and Jewish pioneers in the West. We also found information about early Jewish movie makers. For those of you interested in learning more about Jewish history and the Old West, I recommend a book from the exhibit: *Jewish Life in the American West*, edited by Ava F. Kahn and published by the University of Washington Press.

What surprised both of us most were the wonderful permanent exhibits at the Autry Museum on cowboys and life in the Wild West, including the Wild West shows. We loved the museum so much we returned many times, and you can see how it influenced my story. For those interested in reading more about cowboys, I suggest *The Cowboy*, by Philip Ashton Rollins, published by the University of Oklahoma Press, and *Wild West Shows*, by Paul Reddin, published by the University of Illinois Press.

I knew Rosie would be getting lost in the hills, so we also took a trip into the Santa Monica Mountains. At the visitor's center we found a book called *Wild Heart of Los Angeles: The Santa Monica Mountains*, by Margaret Huffman, published by Roberts Rinehart Publishers. In this book I found invaluable information about flora and fauna, which gave me an idea of what Rosie might encounter out in the hills. But even better than the book was taking a hike one day that took us up into hills just like the ones where Rosie was lost. We saw cat tracks, and it made me a little nervous—I was looking over my shoulder a lot—and I immediately imagined Rosie being chased by a big cat. I even saw a gully just like the one she fell into. After that I was really able to imagine Rosie there.

I also did as much reading as I could about the beginning of the movie industry. I cannot list all the books I used here, but I would suggest for those interested *An Empire of Their Own: How the Jews Invented Hollywood*, by Neal Gabler, published by Anchor Books. There are too many wonderful Internet sites to mention here, but type "silent movies" into a search engine and you'll find a treasure of wonderful information.

I'd like to thank my editor, Jen Weiss, for all her help. She's been wonderful. And thanks to my husband, who went on all the research trips with me, and to my friend Perry Nodelman for letting me run all my ideas past him.

I hope you have enjoyed reading about Rosie's adventures as much as I have enjoyed writing about them.

Warmest wishes,
Carol Matas

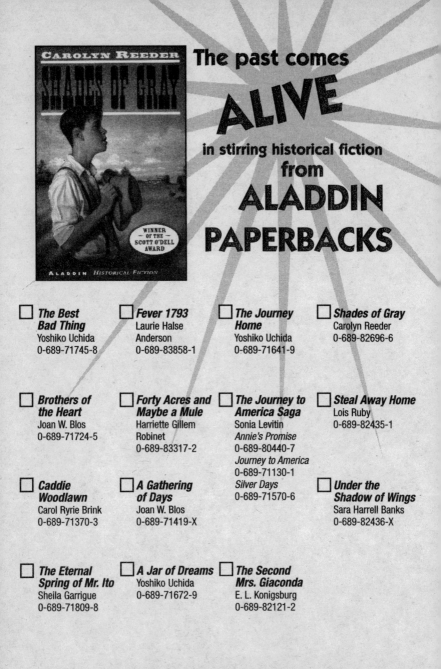

The past comes

ALIVE

in stirring historical fiction

from

ALADDIN PAPERBACKS

☐ **The Best Bad Thing**
Yoshiko Uchida
0-689-71745-8

☐ **Fever 1793**
Laurie Halse Anderson
0-689-83858-1

☐ **The Journey Home**
Yoshiko Uchida
0-689-71641-9

☐ **Shades of Gray**
Carolyn Reeder
0-689-82696-6

☐ **Brothers of the Heart**
Joan W. Blos
0-689-71724-5

☐ **Forty Acres and Maybe a Mule**
Harriette Gillem Robinet
0-689-83317-2

☐ **The Journey to America Saga**
Sonia Levitin
Annie's Promise
0-689-80440-7
Journey to America
0-689-71130-1
Silver Days
0-689-71570-6

☐ **Steal Away Home**
Lois Ruby
0-689-82435-1

☐ **Caddie Woodlawn**
Carol Ryrie Brink
0-689-71370-3

☐ **A Gathering of Days**
Joan W. Blos
0-689-71419-X

☐ **Under the Shadow of Wings**
Sara Harrell Banks
0-689-82436-X

☐ **The Eternal Spring of Mr. Ito**
Sheila Garrigue
0-689-71809-8

☐ **A Jar of Dreams**
Yoshiko Uchida
0-689-71672-9

☐ **The Second Mrs. Giaconda**
E. L. Konigsburg
0-689-82121-2